Rehearsing

A NOVEL BY
MICHAEL CRAFT

For Jim —
With best wishes
and much love.

Michael Craft
2-19-93

Los Hombres Press

REHEARSING

The characters in this story come from the author's imagination. Any resemblance to actual persons, living or dead, is purely coincidental.

Cover and frontispiece drawings by Kevin Hickey.
Typographic design by Mike Johnson.
Author's photo by Tom Zumpano.

Library of Congress Cataloging-in-Publication Data
Rehearsing
ISBN 1-879603-09-8   92-070179

Printed in the United States of America

Copyright © 1993 by Michael Craft

First Edition

        1 2 3 4 5 6 7 8 9 10

Los Hombres Press
P.O. Box 632729
San Diego, CA 92163-2729

To Leon

Rehearsing

MICHAEL CRAFT

PART ONE
Monday Mornings

C L A I R E

I loathe black. This dress does nothing to hide my years; all fifty are exposed to anyone who cares to look. And of course they look. That's why they're here. Their heads are bowed, but mine is erect. I eye them numbly as they peek at my face. They exchange furtive, satisfied glances that say, My God, just look at her, she looks awful. Is Claire Gray really that old? She must be fifty.

I am Claire Gray. You may know of me. The critics say that my name will be a household word after *Traders* opens on Broadway. In theatrical circles, I have been known and respected for many years as a director. But *Traders* is different; I wrote it. The play seems destined for a long, successful run. Some even say it will become a "significant" film.

Standing by a birdbath now, waiting for a fool to finish his prayers, I am the picture of composure, of dignity in grief. But my mind is awash with events and emotions of the past year, with memories of George.

This story begins last summer on a Monday, a spectacular morning in late June when a derelict jumped from the bridge in Central Park. I wasn't rehearsing a show then, but the respite was by no means a vacation. There were meetings with producers and designers, an occasional interview, and scripts to read—always the pile of scripts teetering at the edge of my desk. I intended to read some of them during those quiet summer weeks in the little office that occupies the second bedroom of my apartment, where I have lived alone for many years.

Theater is my life. Forgive the cliché, but a penchant for the dramatic is a symptom of my trade. As you will learn, there are many things I have never understood, and one of these perplexing mysteries is my desire, my *need* to be in a theater, not seated expectantly in the audience, but hard at work.

Work? you ask with a trace of a sneer.

Yes. Creative, life-giving, anxiety-ridden work. Suffice it to say, I'm touchy on this matter, touchy to the point of peevishness. Suffice it to say that on that glorious morning when I was faced with the prospect not of working in a theater, but of enduring another hollow, pointless script in my spare bedroom, I sought escape.

I ride. Granted, I have never understood what would compel an otherwise rational woman to climb onto the back of a horse and subject her loins to a fruitless pounding, but then, there is much I've never understood. Like most horsewomen, I can trace my attraction to the animal back to the prepubescent days of girlhood, an awestruck time of misty eroticism when a powerful bond was fused with the great long-penised steeds.

You are shocked? I too was appalled when the grimy realization first tickled my consciousness. With the passing of years, however, and with the confidence that grows with a maturing mind, I have managed to slough off the assorted nightmares of youth. I have greeted menopause as the long-overdue undoing of puberty itself, and I am happy to report that the loss of my mothering powers has been accompanied by a commensurate loss of some nasty emotional baggage.

It seems I have digressed. Regardless of *why* I ride, it will suffice to note that on that Monday last June I chose not to read scripts in my apartment, but to rent a horse from the public stable and enjoy the morning in the park.

It was nine or ten o'clock. At that hour Central Park is inhabited by a sparse yet diverse array of humanity. The rush hour has ended, and office workers have arrived at their desks. Those who remain in the park are not passing through it; they have come for a personal purpose. Many come to run, escaping the congestion of Manhattan's working streets. Others come to roller skate. It's true: Grown men and women zip along with an earnestness that belies pleasure, perhaps a California phenomenon that has worked its way east. This is yet another mystery I have ceased to contemplate.

There are also homosexuals in the park. An area known as the Ramble is their favorite haunt, I'm told. An outcropping of the island's rocky floor forms a network of steep, winding paths that disappear in the dark foliage. In this quiet maze, men of similar inclination can meet, state their desires with unspoken signals, and act out their fantasies with a crushing of leaves, a snapping of twigs, an occasional ecstatic sigh.

Oddly, the proclivities of these men are not among the mysteries that vex me. Homosexuals are so much a part of my profession—I have dealt with them for so long and in so many ways related to my work—I often feel more comfortable with them than with men I have slept with. Now *there's* a mystery: Is it because I find them witty and charming and talented, or is it a matter of finding homosexuals physically and emotionally unthreatening? Excuse me. They are no longer "homosexuals," of course. They are gay men.

George visited New York each year to see plays. I wonder if he went to the Ramble, if anonymous partners in the leaves moaned at first sight of his horsey endowment.

Ah, yes. Horses. My mount that morning was no pent-up stallion, but a gentle old girl who suited my mood and seemed grateful to escape her confinement. The bridle paths would not suit our quest for freedom—plodding along behind hansom cabfuls of tourists or lovers—so I decided that we'd travel wherever my whim might lead us.

After riding a safe distance from the stable, I turned onto an obscure path, away from the approved cinder trails, which led deep into the park's quiet interior. I halted the horse with a sisterly yank of the reins. She turned her flat, massive head so that one eye peered back at me asking, What's up? I produced an apple. Her eye widened with interest. I explained that the apple was for her if she would promise not to soil the walkways. She flicked her ears in a gesture I chose to interpret as understanding, so I fed her the apple, patting her head while she swallowed. Our pact was sealed.

The park in late June was gloriously verdant. We rode past a species of dwarfed magnolia growing in hidden, unexpected places. Overhead, the foliage of elms, hickories, and sycamores formed a splotchy black matrix against the sky. We traveled for long, serene minutes, emerging onto a narrow path that hugged the craggy perimeter of the Ramble. I reined the horse and looked into the tangle of rocks and trees. In the silence, I strained with vicarious wickedness to hear evidence of the sex-games I imagined being played within. But the only playfulness I detected was that of a breeze, a rustle in the stillness, so we rode on.

Moving south, we arrived at the lake. Its shore was lush with birches and willows, yellow-leaved branches brushing the water's edge. Where the land pinches the water to its narrowest point, an old footbridge spans from shore to shore in a single swoop. Its graceful iron railings have been depicted countless times as a quaint backdrop framing weekend boaters. But this was Monday, and the lake was quiet. I recall no boats, no creaking of oars, no splashing of paddled water.

I had never ridden a horse over the bridge, but its structure was unquestionably sound, and I was feeling adventurous. The only other person in sight was a man who wandered along the opposite shore. His harmlessness was betrayed by an aimless gait, a vacant bearing. So I directed the horse up the sloping bridge. Hooves clopped on the wooden planks as we rose to the top of the arch, then stopped.

Ahead lay Bethesda Fountain. To my right, to the west, just beyond the curtain of trees at the edge of the park, I could glimpse the darting gables and chimneys of the Dakota. For all its prestige, I have never liked this dreary, hulking building. I was especially struck by its gruesomeness that morning as it lurched over the trees to menace the park.

My musing was interrupted by the approach of the man from the opposite shore. I now call him a derelict because he was dressed shabbily, though not in rags. I couldn't read his ageless face beneath several days' growth of beard. He strode up the bridge, approaching me with purpose. I wondered what he wanted, whether he would speak. He stopped about a yard in front of my horse, resting a hand on the side rail. He looked me in the eye and smiled foolishly. I thought he might scold me for riding on the bridge, but he didn't say a word. Instead, he flung his leg over the railing, straddled it a moment, dragged the other leg over, and dropped into the water.

He didn't dive. He didn't leap. He simply dropped into the water with an indelicate splash.

All in all, it was a flawed performance.

As I rode over the bridge toward Bethesda Fountain, I heard no cries for help, no flailing in the water. Fixing my gaze forward, I studied the peeling white bark of a clump birch near the lagoon's edge, trying to bar the disquieting incident from my mind. But I could not. While I generally care little for the opinions of others, I felt relieved that no one was present to condemn my inaction.

I did not even consider trying to save the derelict. I might have been hurt—or worse, killed—and I value my own life far more than a deranged stranger's. Should others brand me as selfish, preferring instead the tenets of unquestioning altruism, they are welcome to their beliefs, and I hope they take comfort in the promise of a final reward.

Anger welled within me as I rode along, stemming not from myself or my inaction, but from the audacity of the man who had darkened my day. Why did he choose me, among Manhattan's millions, to witness his last act? And why did he look at me, smiling so foolishly, just before he jumped?

My frustration mounted, verging on panic, stirred by the anxieties of a lifetime that keep asking, Why so many mysteries? Why all the dark areas that don't seem to fit, the dim little thoughts that itch and nag?

I cantered back to the stable and returned the horse an hour early. "Thanks anyway, old girl," I said while feeding her another apple. "Sorry it didn't work out."

Immersed in my thoughts, I ambled through the park toward the Dakota. My apartment is in the same neighborhood, in the lower West Seventies, off Central Park West. I wondered if Kiki would be waiting there when I arrived.

Kiki Jasper-Plunkett is probably my closest friend. We have known each other since our student days at Evans College, a

Massachusetts girls' school in a picturesque community aptly named Evanstown. The college offers one of the nation's best theater programs, and Kiki says I am its most distinguished alumna. I don't know how she came to this conclusion, but I suspect it contains grains of both flattery and truth.

Upon graduation almost thirty years ago, Kiki left Evans to build a career, but soon returned to the academic nest to enroll in the school's coed graduate program. When she finished her studies, she began to teach at Evans, rising through the ranks, finally arriving at her present position as chairman of the theater department. She is a fine actress and a knowledgeable director. Her passion, however, is costuming.

Kiki has been a frequent visitor to my apartment over the years because her job requires her to keep abreast of New York's theater scene. The purpose of her visit last June, though, was not to see plays, but to tidy up the details of a sabbatical for the coming school year, when she would research the vast costume collection of the Metropolitan Museum. Arrangements were complete, save one. Come fall, Kiki would need a place to live, and she had a plan: She wanted to live in my apartment, which would afford her a short, pleasant commute through the park to the museum on Fifth Avenue.

While Kiki has always been a welcome guest in my home, even for her more extended visits, the prospect of having her move in for a year was untenable to me. The apartment has only one usable bedroom, and I enjoy my privacy. But Kiki had a solution to this problem, too: I was supposed to move out. She contrived a plan by which I would return to Evans, for the first time since graduation, as a guest lecturer, a visiting professor. She wanted us to trade homes.

Since arriving for her visit, she had tried every persuasive tack that her creative mind could devise. Her arguments had been futile because I'd had no interest in returning to Evanstown. But as I walked back from the park, mulling over what had happened on the bridge, I had an idea that brought a sudden spark of interest in Kiki's proposal. My walk slowed to a shuffle as I pieced together the plan. Kiki and I would indeed trade homes for a year.

I glanced at my watch; it was just past twelve. Kiki had surely returned from apartment-hunting. I quickened my pace and emerged from the park onto Central Park West. I crossed the

street and rushed past the Dakota, then turned onto my own
street and climbed the half-flight of stairs to my brownstone. The
door opened before me as I turned two age-worn keys in their
locks. Checking for mail, finding none, I stepped across the hall
to the door of my apartment and paused for a moment while
gathering my thoughts, rehearsing the scene I assumed would
transpire. Should I tantalize Kiki? Should I make her grovel once
more? For the first time since her arrival, I was amused by her
conniving. Two more keys, worn as smooth as the first pair,
opened my door. I stepped inside.

Aware that I would soon be leaving it, I saw my apartment as
if for the first time. I nudged the door closed behind me and
stared at the living room as though I had stumbled into the home
of a stranger. Framed posters—mementos of past triumphs—were
the sole adornment of its stark white walls. At the windows hung
not drapes for their prettiness, but blinds for their privacy. The
furniture was bought on impulse over the years, coordinated by
a vaguely contemporary style. An expanse of bare parquet
stretched underfoot. It was an urban living-space in sharp
contrast to the "vintage" building that contained it. I wondered
how Kiki could possibly adapt to such quarters. I had never seen
her home in Evanstown, but was certain that her tastes were more
cushy than my own.

Kiki had returned and switched on the phonograph. An old
album of show tunes blared so she could hear it from the far
bedroom, where she was undoubtedly changing clothes. Kiki
changes many times a day, a quirky aspect of her passion for
costuming. I crossed the room and adjusted the music to a more
tolerable level, then proceeded to the kitchen.

The events of that morning—the derelict's suicide and my
decision to move from the city—left me parched in a manner that
could be sated only by alcohol. At a corner of the kitchen counter,
a profusion of liquor bottles stood ready, but in deference to the
early hour, I opted for Chardonnay, pouring a glass from the
carafe that was always chilled.

"I *thought* I heard you come in."

Kiki's appearance in the kitchen doorway interrupted my first
sip. My eyes bulged as I swallowed, not in reaction to the wine,
but in an attempt to suppress laughter. While Kiki always dresses
a tad outlandishly, I was unprepared for the spectacle that had

entered my kitchen.

"My God," I blurted, "aren't we a bit long in the tooth for Little Orphan Annie? Forgive my candor, dear, but we *are* the same age, and the 'street-waif look' seems ill suited to our years." Chortling, I wiped wine from my chin.

"How cruel you are." She gasped the words through petulant, pursed lips, tugging at the frayed shawl around her shoulders. I couldn't tell if her getup was meant to portray Miss Doolittle in the opening act of *My Fair Lady* or a homeless urchin from some Dickens tale.

"Kiki," I said flatly, "it's almost July. I don't think you need that . . . wrap. Why don't you take that tattered thing off and have a glass of wine with me?"

"July. January. What's the difference?" she asked in a hopeless whisper, resting her head against the doorjamb, gazing at the ceiling. She let the shawl drop to her feet, revealing a disgusting old sweater with threadbare sleeves.

"For Christ's sake," I snorted, pouring her some wine. "I presume, by this performance, that your morning's search for housing was again fruitless and that you're resigned to spending winter on the streets. Am I close?"

She answered with the slightest nod, suggesting that if she were to speak, she would surely cry. I handed her the wine, which she grasped with both hands, holding it before her chin as a bag lady might clutch a mug of coffee. It took considerable theatrical skill to evoke this image with my best Orrefors crystal.

She looked at me through makeup that made her eyes appear gaunt and sunken. "I've appealed to your pity," she began slowly, choosing her words with care, "but you are unmoved—I haven't shaken your conscience in the least. I've appealed to your career sense by explaining how teaching would broaden and enrich your experience. My God, Claire, I've even coddled your vanity, explaining how you'd become the center of attention at Evans. And still you are unmoved. Still you do not respond."

"I've been responding, Kiki. I've been saying no."

"Claire, Claire. I fervently hoped you wouldn't force me to resort to this." She drew a hefty slug of wine into her mouth and swallowed. Her voice was firmer as she continued, "I want to appeal to your sense of duty."

"Hm," I said. A vacant little expression, it conveyed nothing but my attention. Since Kiki did not continue, I revealed my curiosity by asking, "Duty to what?"

"Why, to Evans, of course. To the school. To the theater program that launched your career."

"Hm."

"There's so much greed in the world," she said in a quiet, dour tone. "Everyone takes, takes, takes. More people should give. That's the essence of duty. You, for instance, took your training from Evans. You have Evans to thank for the career you've enjoyed. Isn't it time to give back . . . "

"Cut the crap, Kiki," I interrupted, neither persuaded nor amused by her logic. "I took my training from Evans, yes. As I recall, I paid some steep tuition for that privilege. That was our agreement, and it was a fair exchange. As for my career, Evans didn't build it; I did. You're a dear old friend, but your reasoning sometimes makes me want to scream—so I take no particular pleasure in telling you that I've decided to go."

"Claire, if it's the money, I can assure you that you would be handsomely compensated at Evans."

"You should listen more carefully, Kiki. I just finished saying that I've decided to move to Evanstown. We'll trade homes as you've suggested."

"Claire, I . . . I," she stammered. Her perplexed expression gave way to a grin as she realized I wasn't joking. "I'm stunned," she said with a little laugh, fidgeting to replenish her wine. "I'd given up hope—I really had."

"Kiki, I'll agree to go, but there's a slight difference to my own plan."

"What is it?" she asked quickly, betraying willingness to reach any compromise I might demand.

"You and I shall trade homes for the year, and I'll join the faculty at Evans. However, I will not teach a full schedule of classes, nor will I direct a full season of plays. Here are my terms: I'm going to Evanstown to give myself time to do some writing. I want to write a play. While working on it, I'll conduct one graduate-level seminar each semester. In the spring, I'll direct one production. It will be my own play if I feel it's any good. You can have my apartment, Kiki—we'll make the switch—if these terms are agreeable."

"Of course, how wonderful!" she gushed without a moment's

consideration. "Look, Claire, I need to get out of these horrid rags. Come talk to me while I change."

Kiki changes moods, as well as her clothes, with uncanny speed and frequency. In the span of two minutes she had pulled herself from the depths of depression and revved herself into a jubilant state that bordered on the manic. She plucked her drink from the countertop and shooed me from the kitchen toward the bedroom. On our way past the phonograph, she broke stride long enough to flip the record, and the apartment was again filled with the strains of a boppy production number. She danced into the bedroom and flung open the closet doors. I parked myself in the doorway, chuckling while she fingered through her wardrobe, tossing items onto my bed for inspection.

"Whatever changed your mind?" she asked. "You went to the park for a ride this morning, right? I knew it would be good for you—the way you moped around the apartment last week, reading scripts. It did you good to get out, I guess."

"That's not what sparked my decision," I said softly while swirling the wine in my glass. "Something happened in the park. I witnessed a suicide."

"Oh, how sad," she said with only a trace of concern as she scrutinized the match of a sweater with a pair of slacks. "And when you saw this," she continued, "you felt the city had gone crazy, so you decided that a year in the country would be good for your mental health. Is that it?"

"No, Kiki, it wasn't like that at all. I've wanted to write my own play for a long time—I suppose every director wants to show the world how to do it properly—but I never knew what to 'say.' Now it's clear to me. After what happened this morning, everything fell into place."

"Suicide seems a rather morbid inspiration. Is that what your play will be about?"

"No, Kiki. I'm still at a loss to tell you anything about the play's plot, but I do know its message. I've even decided on a title, since it sums up the theme so well."

"All right," she said with a patronizing air. "I'll bite: What will be the name of your play?"

"*Traders.*"

"Traitors? It's about political misconduct?"

"No, Kiki. *Traders,* with a *d.* It's about relationships."

To me this explanation seemed complete and self-evident, but Kiki appeared mystified by it. She stopped fussing with her clothes and eyed me with raised brows, expecting me to continue. But I had nothing more to say, forcing me to wonder how I would expand my thematic idea into a hundred-page script.

When it became clear that I would offer no insights, Kiki said, "You're going to write about relationships, about traders. People trading things, right? I get it," she said as her features relaxed. "People involved in relationships become traders—like us, trading homes for a year."

"You've got the idea, Kiki. But it runs a bit deeper."

A chivalrous escort, Hector Bosch walked at my side, guiding me through the after-theater traffic with a delicate grasp of my elbow. Only when we arrived at the restaurant did he drop his arm from mine, reaching to open the door.

"Good evening, Miss Gray," said the attractive young host as I entered. "It's been far too long."

I smiled but said nothing, as I could not recall that we'd met.

"And Mr. Bosch," he continued, "a pleasant evening to you, sir. Your usual table is waiting."

Hector bantered with the man while removing the Burberry that was draped from his shoulders. Finding the evening warm, I hadn't worn a coat at all. But Hector chose to keep his silk scarf, explaining that he found the air conditioning drafty. In truth, he couldn't bear to part with the scarf because its foulard matched his necktie as well as the wisp of a handkerchief peeking from his breast pocket.

Hector seated me, then the host seated Hector. I ordered kir, which was trendy that summer, and Hector ordered his "usual." We sat silently for a moment while Hector craned to glimpse anyone he might have overlooked during our entrance.

As his eyes darted about the room, he fussed with the knot of his tie and stroked his moustache, sprouted some years ago to compensate for the crescent of forehead growing steadily deeper into his hairline. He is one of the most fastidious dressers I've ever known. His mannerisms might seem uncomfortably effeminate to someone unexposed to the theater crowd, but his bedtime yens are decidedly heterosexual, as he has demonstrated over the years during our occasional conjugations. For reasons that baffle me, he has proposed marriage often. For reasons that baffle him, I have never been tempted to accept. Hector Bosch is a friend. He is also the most respected theater critic in New York.

When our drinks arrived, he asked, "What did you think of the play, my dear?" His sonorous coo broke into a chuckle as he raised his glass in a toast.

It was Wednesday night, two days after the derelict jumped from the bridge. We'd come from a play that would be the subject of Hector's next column in the New York *Weekly Review*. He was surprised when I accepted his invitation, since I rarely accompany him on "working evenings." Critics and directors tend, after all, to be natural antagonists. I'd agreed to be his guest that night, however, because I was eager to talk to him about my plans for the coming year.

The play we saw was *Broken Toys*, a self-indulgent bit of sophistry dreamed up by some obscure academic. It had found its way to New York, previewing Off Broadway only a few blocks from the restaurant where we now sat.

"It was lousy," I told him, unwilling to pass judgment more eloquently. I tipped the little glass and tasted the kir.

"Lousy? Is that all you can say about a work so rife with social import?" Hector's tone was serious, almost scolding, but his grin betrayed facetiousness. He tasted his drink. The tip of his tongue darted with reptilian efficiency to wipe droplets of liquor from the edge of his moustache. "I wish you'd be more specific, my dear. How can I stretch 'lousy' into the sort of meaningful review that my readers expect?"

"Hector," I explained, "that's your problem. If you care to waste your ink as well as your time detailing why the play is lousy—a play upholding incest as the ultimate expression of love—I have no particular interest in dissuading you. Why did you choose to review it in the first place?"

"Oh, I don't know, Claire," he said with a frustrated wave of his hand. "It's been such a miserable summer. I've seen nothing that's worth the price of a ticket. If the current dearth of substantial theater weren't so pathetic, I swear I'd find the situation funny. But I find no humor in it."

"Come now, Hector. You're known and loved for your stinging wit. I should think *Broken Toys* would be just what the doctor ordered to perk up a dull summer."

"For God's sake," he snapped, "how can I possibly make light of incest and child abuse? Even from me, it wouldn't wash." He again drank, this time wiping his moustache with the length of an index finger, which he then scrubbed with his napkin. "Brighten my evening, Claire," he said in a different tone, much softer, almost pleading. "Brighten my next column. Tell me what to expect from you next season. You've cloistered yourself for the last few weeks reading scripts, yet you haven't said a peep about your next production. Have you reached a decision, Claire?"

"I knew it," I said with dry humor. "I didn't think you asked me out tonight for the mere pleasure of my company. I assumed you had an ulterior motive."

"Naturally," he admitted without shame as he brushed a fleck of something from his tie. "I may not be the most conventional journalist, but I do have a nose for news. I have wined you—and am about to dine you—because I want the scoop."

I snorted a wry laugh, pleased that he would resort to such dreadful jargon as "scoop." Amused that my intentions could tantalize him so, I sipped my kir before telling him casually, "I *have* reached a decision that your readers may find interesting. May I have a cigarette?"

He produced a Gauloise from a flat silver case and a speck of flame from a matching lighter. "Yes, Claire? A decision?" he asked with strained patience.

Inhaling the first drag of unfiltered smoke, so acridly French, I settled back in my chair. "I agree with you, Hector. There has indeed been a dearth of significant theater lately—barring my own contributions, of course." I smiled.

"Of course." He mirrored my smile.

"And I spent the last few weeks in search of the script that could turn this trend around. But I did not find it. I am forced, therefore, to turn to the work of a first-timer."

"What?" he asked, astonished. "Claire Gray—directing the work of an unknown playwright?"

"The author is quite well known, though not as a playwright." I leaned forward, looking into his eyes to tell him, "Hector, I am the author. The play is called *Traders*. But it's not written yet. I'll need a year to get it to Broadway, if in fact I write it, if I feel it's any good."

Hector's lips twitched as if he were about to speak, but he was too confused to formulate a question. I spared him the trouble and explained my arrangement with Kiki.

Eventually he said, "I never knew you were an Evans girl. Impressive. The cachet of a degree from Evans has launched more than one career in this business." After a moment's thought, he asked, "What did you say you'll call the play?"

"*Traders*. It's about . . . trading."

"Trading what?"

"Everything."

Hector sat quietly, rubbing a finger around the rim of his empty glass. He smiled, hailed our waiter, and ordered more drinks. Then he reached across the table for my hand.

"I don't fully understand what you're up to," he told me, "but I've learned to trust your judgment. I hope you do it, Claire. No one alive has a finer sense of staging. If you can transform your talent for interpreting a script into a talent for creating one, your play will be well worth the wait. But such a wait! My dear, how you tax us," he complained with an exaggerated pout. "Now tell me, how did you reach this decision? Have you always wanted to write a play?"

"I've often thought of it—who in our business hasn't? But it wasn't until Monday morning that I took the idea seriously. While riding a horse in the park, I saw a derelict jump from the footbridge into the lagoon. There was an item in yesterday's paper."

"Good God, how awful, Claire. Then what?"

"He drowned, of course."

"But what did *you* do?"

"I rode my horse back to the stable, then walked home. That's when I decided to return to Evanstown."

"Surely you didn't ride away until after you'd determined you couldn't save the poor wretch."

"I doubt that I could have saved him, but I didn't stick around to find out. He didn't cry for help, if that's any consolation to you."

"Claire, I . . . I hope you're not telling me that you turned your back on this pathetic soul in his moment of greatest need."

"I'm sorry if this disturbs you, Hector, but the man was deranged and wanted to die. And I don't swim very well."

Hector shook his head with disappointment. "I've always admired your fierce independence, but I never suspected it was a symptom of deeper traits. Do you realize, Claire, that most people would say you behaved selfishly?"

"Hm."

"Say it's not so, my dearest. Tell me of the great distance from which you witnessed this tragedy, a distance that negated any possibility of your aid."

"Quite to the contrary, the man stood as near to me then as you're sitting now." I patted Hector's hand as proof of our proximity. "He looked me in the eye, climbed over the rail, and dropped into the water. That's all there was to it."

"You're toying with me," he said slyly. "First you say you were riding a horse. Now you tell me the man on the bridge stood within reach of you. You really ought to keep your story straight." Hector laughed openly, certain he had trapped me. "Which was it? Were you on a horse or were you on the bridge?"

"I was riding the horse *over* the bridge."

"But that's a pedestrian bridge," he said, incredulous. "How could you ride a horse across it? That's not permitted."

"For God's sake, Hector, you've become exceptionally tiresome this evening. I had no idea you would react this way, and I'm sorry if I've upset you. There—the matter is closed."

"Very well. It rests on your conscience, not mine. But I'm curious, Claire. What ran through your mind?"

"I was angry, Hector—mad as hell. I was mad at the derelict for spoiling my ride. I was mad at the crap people believe, mad that I should have to explain my motives for riding away from a messy and dangerous situation—sane, rational motives that shouldn't require a syllable of justification. And I'm mad now that you would saddle me with guilt for the sake of padding your own altruistic fantasies. I'm getting old, Hector, and you're a few years older. Isn't it time we both grew up?"

He watched as I spoke, intrigued by my anger. As moments passed, his eyes probed mine. When at last he spoke, his tone was soft, not scolding. "I assume you understand your own words, Claire, but I'll be damned if I can grasp them."

"I'm only beginning to understand. So much began to make sense as I rode away from that man. Don't you see? That's why I'm going to Evanstown."

"No, I don't see," he said with a bemused sigh. "I thought you decided to write the play because you wanted a decent script to direct."

"Certainly, that's part of it. After directing other people's work for thirty years, spending my career bringing their words and thoughts to life, I finally reached the point where I was tired of mediocrity and second-guessing. Take a hard look at the play we saw tonight. How would you like to open a script and be faced with the pointless challenge of interpreting something like that? Yes, frustration is part of the reason I want to write, but there's much more."

"Very well, Claire," he said with a smile. "Go with my blessing and write *Traders*—not that I could stop you. Are you getting hungry?"

"Yes, Hector. I need meat."

I did need meat. It was well after eleven, and the two kirs had functioned admirably as an apéritif, stimulating great hunger as well as pleasant light-headedness.

Hector signaled to our waiter that we were ready to order, then settled back in his chair to study the wine list.

Toward the end of the meal—it was nearly one o'clock—Hector leaned forward to refill my glass and said in a low voice, barely above a whisper, "You know, my dearest, since you will be leaving town soon, and since you will be away for such a very long time, and since it's getting rather late, it might be . . . fitting . . . that we spend the night together."

"Hm."

My expression was noncommittal, but my desire was betrayed by the arch of my brows, a signal Hector decoded with ease.

"My place or yours?" he asked, dispensing with all other preliminaries.

"Yours. I have a house guest," I reminded him, then added with a wink, "though I'm sure Kiki would be delighted to watch."

"My place will do nicely," he assured me.

That was almost a year ago. The night was enjoyable yet unremarkable. Hector performed energetically, and I reciprocated to his satisfaction. I assume Hector and I will enjoy each other's company again soon. It is long overdue.

But it will never be the same—not since George.

Kiki returned to Evanstown over the weekend, and I looked forward to a quiet day at home when I could deal with the growing list of details to be resolved before leaving New York. But Monday morning brought a stream of phone calls.

The *Weekly Review* had arrived in the mail. Hector's column appeared in its usual space on the tabloid's front page. A striking photo of Hector grinned at his readers from the top of the article. I could be charitable and call the picture flattering, making Hector look five years younger than he is. In truth, it was taken more than ten years ago and has run with his column ever since.

I did not expect to find my own picture in print that morning, but there it was. Like Hector's, my photo was at least ten years old. Unlike his, mine was neither striking nor flattering.

The column had prompted the phone calls. I sat at the desk in my extra bedroom, coffee and smoking paraphernalia arrayed before me, with the telephone receiver nestled between shoulder and ear. The *Review* lay near the side of the desk, tossed against the pile of unread scripts, with my picture staring back at me upside down. I reached for the paper and, turning it aright, skimmed through the column again while listening to my caller.

TRADERS FOR BROKEN TOYS?
NY Theatergoers to Face Long, Dark Season
By Hector Bosch
Senior Critic-at-Large

If *Broken Toys,* which previewed Off Broadway last week, is any indication of what New Yorkers can expect from the fall season of theatrical offerings, I am forced to conclude that serious playgoers will be weighing three options: (1) attend revivals of old favorites, (2) stay home, or (3) move to Chicago.

Uninviting as these prospects may seem, they are vastly preferable to enduring a play of the caliber of *Broken Toys.* We have seen many bad plays, but never have we been subjected to one that so actively assaults the sensitivity, good taste, and common decency of its audience.

The play is in two acts, set somewhere in the deepest South. Act One culminates with the rape by an itinerant farm worker of his twin eight-year-old daughters. The farmer, dubbed "Pappy," accomplishes this deed with the aid of some highly sophisticated bondage techniques. We found the staging to be uncomfortably explicit, and while we have always been a vocal opponent of artistic censorship, we were forced to wonder why the theater had not been raided.

In Act Two, the girls philosophize about the trauma that has befallen them. Quoth Maggie: "Gosh, Ellie, I don't know *what* to think." Ellie replies: "I do, Maggie. I think Pappy's just showin' he loves us the best way he knows how. 'Member how he always used to call us his 'pretty little toys'? Well, now we're just [*pause*] now we're just our Pappy's broken toys." With these enlightened words, gentle reader, the curtain mercifully falls.

There was one bright spot, however, to recoup this otherwise dismal loss of an evening. Seated at my side was Claire Gray, Broadway's unrivaled first lady of directing. Supping together after the play, she revealed to this reporter some startling professional plans.

Alas, it is our sad duty to report that Claire Gray will direct no Broadway shows next season. She will in fact leave New York for a year.

Hollywood, you surmise? It is no secret that Miss Gray has been courted recently by emissaries of the television and motion picture industries. We daresay she could contribute much to these media, but her response to these magi from the West is well known. Claire Gray's career, loyalty and passion rest solely in the legitimate theater.

What, you ask, could entice Claire Gray away from Manhattan? Her mission is a noble one. Not content with past successes, not content with her status as *prima donna assoluta* of the directing world, not content with the quality of scripts that are daily presented for her consideration, Claire Gray has decided to write her own play.

She has accepted a one-year appointment to the theater faculty of Evans College, her alma mater. She will carry a light teaching load, devoting most of her time to writing. If satisfied with her efforts, she will direct the play at Evans next spring, then open it on Broadway in the fall.

It is tempting to speculate about the leading role she will undoubtedly write for Arnold Manley, but such musings are premature, for Miss Gray informs us that the play's plot is still unknown. Her inspiration is essentially thematic, and the theme is reflected in the title she has chosen: *Traders.*

So hold onto your playbills. We're in for a rough ride next season without Claire Gray's directorial talents gracing our stages. Let us wish her *bon chance* in Massachusetts. Let us hope that idyllic Evanstown will inspire her to write the kind of script she wants, the kind of play we need.

Hector Bosch has spoken.

I chuckled aloud as I read the last line, which Hector uses to close every column.

"What's so funny?" Arnold Manley asked me over the phone. "I wasn't kidding. I think it's a wonderful idea."

"Sorry, Manny. I wasn't laughing at you. I was glancing at Hector's column."

"I've seen it, of course. Everyone has. You really know how to set things buzzing." His rhythm was excited, his tone sincere. The inflections were unmistakably those of the young actor destined to become an overnight sensation, Hollywood's next heartthrob. But I hadn't chosen to nurture Arnold Manley's career for reasons of physical attraction. I became his mentor because I recognized his talent. In his late twenties, approaching the maturity of thirty, he breathed life into his acting with a vision well beyond his years. I patiently coached him, casting him in roles that let him learn as well as perform. Then came *Inner Moments.* I directed and Manny played the lead, his first on Broadway, which brought him to the attention of critics on both coasts. I was grooming him for something, but I didn't realize until reading Hector's column that I had trained Arnold Manley for one purpose—to play the lead in *Traders.*

". . . the reason I'm calling," he continued. "I have some news of my own. It's about *Inner Moments.*"

"Oh?" I said coyly, having expected his "news" for weeks. "You've signed a movie contract? Rumors have been rampant."

"I know, Claire. But I wanted you to hear it from me.

Production begins soon. I'll be leaving for California around the time you leave for Evanstown."

"But *who*, Manny?"

"Fedders is both directing and producing."

"Good," I said with a breath of relief. "You couldn't have done better. He's the best in the business."

"You're not angry?" he asked sheepishly. "Everyone knows how you feel about Hollywood."

"Listen, Manny." I paused to collect my thoughts. "I have opinions, for my own reasons, and they apply to *my* career. I gave you your start for a purely selfish motive: You made me look good. But I can't expect you to spend your whole life as my protégé. I'm not so entangled in this cloak of 'legitimate theater' that I can't appreciate what you've accomplished. How many thirty-year-old actors get snatched from Broadway after one leading role, by a producer of Fedders' stature, to star in a major film? Angry, darling? I'm delighted. So go make your movie." I paused a beat, then suggested, "But if you feel you owe me something, you can promise one thing."

"What's that?" he asked, then added with a laugh, ". . . as if I couldn't guess."

"Hector Bosch is as insightful as he is shrewd. This morning's column suggests that I'll write you a role in *Traders*. Manny, the principal role will be tailored for you. Will you play it for me and bring my words to life? Not in Evanstown, of course—you're far too big for that now. But if I bring the show to Broadway, will you star in it?"

"Of course," he replied without hesitation. "I'd be furious if you wrote the part for anyone else. You've never led me astray, and I'm sure you won't now. Will I see you soon?"

"I hope so. Parting ways for a year, we ought to mark the occasion. I'll phone you when I figure out my schedule. Good-bye, Manny, and best of luck."

"Same to you, dear lady."

I hung up the phone and stared at the newspaper with a satisfied smile. I could predict Manny's success with *Inner Moments*, and I was pleased to hear his commitment to *Traders*. I lifted my cup and sipped the coffee I'd neglected, but it was tepid, so I reached for a cigarette instead. The phone rang. I exhaled with a weary sigh that asked, Now what? On the second ring, I plucked the still-warm receiver from its cradle and planted it in the crook of my neck. "Yes?"

"Good morning, my dear. You've been difficult to reach. I presume you've seen the column?"

"Yes, Hector. It seems all Manhattan has seen your column. I hope that pleases you."

"Indeed it does. And don't try to tell me it doesn't please you as well. A little extra attention never hurts, does it? A stroking of the old ego can be very pleasant."

"I suppose I should thank you, Hector, but I have a ton of things to do before I leave, and all this ego-stroking, quite frankly, is getting in the way. I'm starting to question the sanity of the whole idea."

"Then scrap it, Claire. Stay here and marry me. A big church wedding—fall weddings can be so lovely—*the* social event of the year. Imagine the cachet of a Bosch-Gray union!"

Hector's proposals frequently came without warning, so his mawkish spontaneity failed to surprise me. I answered with my usual empty "Hm."

"Why can't you take me seriously?" he pouted.

"I take you seriously," I assured him. "I simply don't want to marry. I've made it this far. Christ, Hector, why screw things up now?"

"Claire!" he admonished me, genuinely shocked. "Marriage is the holiest of unions."

"You should know, Hector, having weathered three holy unions. Thank you, but no. Besides, I can't change plans now—'Hector Bosch has spoken,' remember? We wouldn't want to disappoint your readers."

"No, no. Quite right," he admitted, satisfying me that the topic of matrimony had been sidestepped. "Anyway, dearest, the reason I called. When are you leaving for Massachusetts?"

"I'll take a short trip next week to scout around. I'll move there in a month, the first of August."

"I see," he said, as if taking notes. "I want to throw a party, a *bon voyage* affair. How about . . . ," he paused a moment, clicking a ball-point pen. "How about the last Saturday of July? Your last weekend in New York."

"That sounds delightful," I told him. Hector is known as a model host. His parties are notorious, his invitations coveted.

"When should I plan my entrance—eight or nineish?"

"Nineish."

"I have a thought, Hector. Do you intend to invite Arnold Manley?"

"Certainly, assuming he's available. I'm sure he'll want to wish you well in this new phase of your work."

"Perhaps the party should be for both of us. People will want to wish *him* well too, you know."

Hector was silent, so I asked, "You've heard about *Inner Moments*, haven't you? Manny has signed with Fedders."

"When?" His flat inflection betrayed mild panic.

"I presume it was over the weekend or even this morning. He told me on the phone just before you called."

"Drat!"

I laughed at his stuffy oath. "What's wrong, Hector?"

"I should have known about this. It's a whole week before my next column appears."

"Perhaps you should go back to the *Times*. You could write your heart out every day."

"No, thank you. I joined the *Review* to rid myself of that grind. But here I am, sitting on the hottest theatrical news since . . . well, since my scoop about your year at Evans. My second major story in one day, and I have no way to print it."

"It's feast or famine, darling."

"Don't you understand? Someone else may break the story before I can. I really must go," he said abruptly. "I'll call Arnold right away. Maybe the story'll keep—who knows?"

"Who knows?" I repeated, suspecting that Manny's story couldn't possibly keep for a week. It would in fact appear in the next edition of the *Times*.

"We're set for the last Saturday in July?" he asked.

"Yes, dear, all set. The party sounds marvelous. B'bye."

I hung up the phone, glanced again at Hector's column, then peered at the scummy brown ring that had formed in my coffee cup. I decided that a rinse and a refill were in order. As I pushed my chair from the desk and stood, the phone rang. I groaned, slumping back into the chair to answer with a dull "Yes?"

It was my mother calling from her home upstate.

"Yes, mother, I have been on the phone all morning. No, I haven't been gabbing—I've been answering calls. I suppose you saw Hector's column. All true, every word. And I must admit I'm getting excited about returning to Evanstown—it's been almost thirty years. Yes, I realize our visits will be easier, and you know you're always welcome. Hm. Of course, as soon as I get settled. Hector? Oh, he reacted with mixed emotions—he explained them well enough in his column. Yes, it was sweet of him. Uh, yes, he did call this morning. Yes, mother, he did 'ask me' again, but I really don't care to discuss it. Mother, there's nothing more to be said. Yes, dear, I know. Well, it was so nice of you to call. We don't have enough of these little chats. I will, I promise. You too, dear. B'bye."

Replacing the receiver, I unplugged the phone, grabbed the cup and saucer, and headed for the kitchen.

As I stood at the sink rinsing the cup, my eyes wandered to the clock. It was nearly noon; the entire morning had slipped away. Mother's call had upset me, and I thought of the carafe of chilled wine. But I warned myself that I had much to accomplish that afternoon and settled for more coffee. As I took the first sip, I realized that unplugging the telephone at my desk would not prevent the kitchen wall phone from ringing, and I cringed at the thought of more intrusions. So I reached for the receiver and placed a call of my own.

"Good afternoo-oon," lilted a receptionist's voice. "Theater department, Evans College."

"Good afternoon. Is Doctor Jasper-Plunkett in?"

"She's terribly busy right now," the girl informed me with an officious air. "Could she return your call after lunch?"

"Please ask her to phone Claire Gray."

"Claire Gray?" the girl repeated, her tone now flustered. "Certainly, Miss Gray. I mean, please hold the line, and I'll connect you."

Waiting several seconds, I listened to the electronic limbo stretching between Manhattan and the Berkshires.

"Claire!" said Kiki with an emphasis that could have sprung from either delight or consternation. "I'm so glad you called. I've been trying to reach you all day."

"My phone hasn't stopped ringing since Hector's article appeared this morning."

"Neither has mine. This office has been a madhouse, a veritable zoo, darling, and I haven't even seen the column. I know this sounds rather mysterious, but all our copies seem to be missing. Just what did Hector say?"

"Well, he began by reviewing a real dog of a play we saw last week, then he broke the news about my coming to Evans. That's all there was to it."

"My God, Claire, I don't think you realize the impact of news like that on a town like this. Evanstown is extremely theater-conscious, and it wasn't empty flattery when I called you our most distinguished alumna. It may be the dead of summer, but sleepy little Evanstown is suddenly humming."

"Sorry to have caused such a stir," I lied, delighted to hear the effect of the news.

"I love it," said Kiki. "We've had calls from students every-where wanting to transfer into our program, which is impossible, and telegrams from our own students requesting to enroll in your seminars. And then there's the mayor, who's waiting in my inner office. We were talking when you called. He's offered city funds to help produce your play in the spring—if casting is open to the community theater group and if the show is produced in their playhouse."

"What do you think?"

"It sounds good. The Evanstown Players is a splendid local group. We often draw upon them for our own productions—the college has no undergraduate men, remember."

"I remember."

"As for their playhouse, we'd probably want to use it anyway. It's newer and bigger than the school's, and your play is bound to be a quick sellout. There's no obligation to cast any of the locals, just audition them. You'll be pleasantly surprised; they've got some fine talent. There's George . . . "

"Kiki," I interrupted, "is the mayor aware that I may not produce *Traders*? It may never get written."

"Yes, dear. He's so excited, he'd agree to anything. The whole town's excited! There's even talk that Arnold Manley may come to Evans to star in your play."

Amazed at how quickly the idea had spread, I explained, "Hector speculated in his article that I'd write a role for Manny. That's all that's been said in print."

"In print," she repeated, her voice laced with suspicion. "But privately, Claire?"

"Privately," I stressed, "Manny and I do have an agreement. Yes, he will play my leading role on Broadway if the project goes that far, so I'll use your local talent for the Evanstown premiere. And bear in mind, these plans are confidential."

"Strictly *entre nous*, of course, dear."

"Speaking of plans, Kiki—the reason I'm calling—I'd like to come up next week. Just a short visit, a day or two to look around and reorient myself."

"How marvelous. There are no direct flights, but there's always the train. The 8:32 leaves New York every morning. It takes a few hours, but it's a quiet ride, and you travel through some beautiful country. I'll arrange a big welcome."

"No, Kiki, please don't. Returning to Evanstown is bound to be emotional for me. I'd prefer to keep it low-key."

"I understand. When would you like to come?"

"How about Monday, a week from today?"

"I'll be waiting at the train," she assured me, then added, "Do be a lamb and bring a copy of today's *Weekly Review*. We're all dying to read Hector's column."

"Fine, if I remember," I said vacantly. "But I don't understand what happened to your copy. Aren't there others you could read there at school?"

"There aren't, Claire. That's what makes this whole thing so goofy. Our secretary says the papers arrived this morning and were distributed to our mailboxes. Later, the papers weren't there. So we called the college library, which carries a subscription. Same thing. Their copy arrived, they stamped it in, and an hour later it was missing. Isn't that queer? It sounds as if someone in town didn't want anyone to read Hector's column. But that doesn't make sense, does it?"

Next Monday morning, the 8:32 was almost empty. I was the only passenger in my car. A surly conductor sauntered through to take my ticket, informing me that if I wished to smoke, I would have to move to the smoker at the far end of the train. Grudgingly, I stamped out my cigarette on the linoleum floor. When he had gone, I lit another and peered through the window.

The city crept slowly away. I watched the dreary switchyard disappear in a tunnel's blackness, then squinted as the train emerged into the stark light and shadow of deep urban canyons. Buildings soon parted, and we clattered across long steel bridges, leaving Manhattan with the murky water behind us. Residential sprawl gave way to industrial sprawl, which in turn gave way to the first few snatches of green, open land. These bits of countryside grew and spread until at last the train was streaking through a vast panorama of endless vegetation under white summer sky.

The noise of the train was itself a kind of silence—the droning silence of metal wheels engaging metal rails—the deafening man-made silence of great diesel engines. I slipped into its void. My eyes absorbed the sameness of the landscape, yet saw nothing. I dreamed, but never slept. I cannot say how long I drifted in this peaceful state; it seemed as though hours had been compressed into an instant. And then I thought of mother.

I blinked.

She had sneaked into my mind and yanked me from my reverie. I searched the landscape for familiar features, but found none, save a cluster of spires in the distant hills, a vague reminder of the town where I grew up, the town where my mother still lives. Was it the setting that turned my thoughts to her? Or was I still, perhaps, in a subliminal tiff over her phone call of the previous Monday?

I'm not openly hostile toward mother. I treat her kindly at best, respectfully at worst. I've learned not to address her criticisms, argue her beliefs, or play her games. My only defense against her loving attacks is a buffer of nonchalance, so I call her "dear" and "darling" as though we were great old chums. I perform the required visits. We chatter like schoolgirls until she starts probing my past, questioning my future, harping about marriage—and I announce that the discussion is closed.

I continued to gaze through the window, mulling over my thoughts, not reacting to the things I saw, never flinching as trees rushed toward the train and swept past me. I was lost again in the hum of the engine, in the soothing rocking of the floor beneath me. I was lulled into another waking dream.

It began as a nagging germ of an idea that throbbed with the pulse of the rails, a sore that would grow within me and burst. But the pain began so gently, the thought nudged my brain so slowly and was born so serenely, I was taken unaware by the foretaste of my mother's death.

Mystics and dreamers may question death's grip, but I do not. I've long known death as an intellectual reality, but it never once scratched my emotions till I pondered the surety of my own mother's passing. I am fifty years old; my mother is nearly eighty. While healthy and alert, she is living beyond her time. Any day, I could face the task of burying her.

The facts of life and death become apparent to any farsighted person while slipping into middle age. The inescapable is more imminent with each passing year, month, hour. My thoughts on the train were startling not because they were new, but because of their clarity. I didn't picture my mother's death scene in a clairvoyant sense, but I did see what it would mean to me.

I would be free.

It's an uneasy admission—something of a confession—that so grievous a loss can be sweetened by the lure of freedom. I have no reason to wish her dead. She doesn't live with me; she hasn't turned mean or senile; I haven't known the horrors of those who must nurse their failing parents. Yet the thought I could not suppress was this: There is a woman out there, somewhere among the billions, who claims me as hers. I may be fifty, but I am hers. No one else can cripple me with such physical ties, such emotional bonds.

I want loose.

I wanted loose that morning on the train. I saw with sudden insight that I would be free, I would be my *self*, only at the moment of my mother's death. Burying her would be my ultimate act of maturity, my last rite of passage into adulthood.

As the train pulled into town, I glimpsed views that transported me back thirty years to my student days. Evanstown resembles any number of quaint New England towns, except for its unique setting. Evans Run—not really a stream, but a sizable river—cuts a valley north and south between two ridges of the Appalachian foothills. The Lower Ridge consists of grassy knolls; the Upper Ridge, to the west, is mountainous. On the slopes of the Upper Ridge, both Evanstown and Evans College were founded on the same day in 1818. The train hissed to a crawl at the station. I remembered a functional, uninspired building without claim to style or prettiness. What I now saw looked like a movie set. A gingerbread affair with schoolhouse-red siding and green enameled shutters, its fanciful gables rose to a clocked cupola topped with a weather vane. As the train lurched to a stop, I expected a dancing chorus of man-sized mice or rabbits to emerge from the door of the storybook station to greet me. Instead, Kiki emerged wearing a bright summer frock.

Stepping from the train to the platform, I could see the once-familiar landmarks of Evans College stacked on the slopes of the Upper Ridge, surrounded by the houses and shops of the town. In the high-noon sunlight that cast no shadows, the buildings and trees on the side of the mountain looked like a backdrop for *Our Town*, a naive, sentimental painting by an artist untutored in the laws of perspective.

If the town in the distance seemed unreal, the reality of my arrival was confirmed by the smack of Kiki's lips on my cheek. "Claire, darling," she gushed. "Welcome home."

"Thank you, dear," I told her, returning her kiss, pecking low to avoid smudging the rouge.

"My God!" she said in sudden panic, pointing to the departing train. "The rest of your things . . . "

"No, Kiki," I laughed. "This is all I brought." I hoisted my little duffle, an overnight bag that could pass for a large purse.

She shook her head, amazed that I could travel without luggage. Taking the duffle, she led me around the station to the parking lot, chattering all the way. A wristful of bracelets jangled in rhythm with her stride.

"Here we are," she announced, tossing the bag behind the two seats of a convertible sports car. "What do you think?"

It was an English roadster, exceedingly cute, predictably red. It looked like a toy next to the dollhouse depot. "It's charming," I said with feigned enthusiasm as we took our seats. I am not a tall woman, so I had to wonder—sitting in the passenger's seat with my knees pressed immodestly against my chest—what compelled Kiki to buy a machine seemingly engineered for human discomfort.

"You'll take good care of my baby, won't you?" she asked. "It goes with the house."

"I don't drive," I told her while forcing my feet into the dark recess beneath the glove compartment.

She started the engine and pulled out of the lot, asking, "You won't mind keeping it while I'm away, will you? Maybe you could ask a friend to take it out for a spin now and then."

"If I make any friends."

"What nonsense!" she scolded. "The whole town is dying to meet you. In fact, there are two people whom you *must* meet today, or my job is in peril. Doddson Clark Henry is president of the college, and Constance Garamond is head of the English department."

"Hm."

"Keep in mind, Claire, that you'll be employed by the school, and Dody and Connie outrank you. It's important to hit it off with them from the start."

"Welcome to academia . . . ," I muttered as the car spun around a corner and climbed one of the streets leading to campus. My words were barely audible over an anguished downshifting of gears.

I had never seen Kiki drive before, and her fervor surprised me. I stared at her hand on the stick shift, knuckles blanched, fingers splayed. "Now, Claire," she said in a consoling tone while punching the clutch with her foot, "Dody and Connie are awfully sweet people, utterly charming. You'll get along famously, I'm sure."

"I'm sure," I said without inflection. Our words had grown trivial. I was absorbed in my surroundings.

My memories of Evanstown focused on winter, for I'd never set foot there in summer. I remembered the icy walks, the northwest winds that swept down from the Upper Ridge to pile drifts at the door overnight, the Saturday toboggan parties on the slopes, the grog parties afterward. Now I was transfixed by the green, quiet beauty of the town. Kiki mentioned new buildings and old friends while our open car zipped along brick-cobbled streets beneath a leafy tunnel of tall, arching branches.

"Know where we are?" Kiki asked.

"How could I forget?" I replied with a little laugh. "Beacon Street. Yeats House is ahead."

There are no beacons in Evanstown. The street's notable namesake was meant to lend a cosmopolitan air to this outpost of arts and letters. The most prestigious addresses in town are on Boston Drive, known among the students as Professors Row.

There are no dormitories or sororities at Evans. Undergraduate girls live in comfortable old houses that forge many lifelong friendships. I lived with Kiki at Yeats House.

She braked the car and parked at the curb with the engine running. "Look about the same?" she asked.

"It does," I said softly. "The trees are bigger, but the house is exactly as I remember it." A hulk of a building with just enough detail to qualify as Georgian, it squatted atop a hill that rose from the sidewalk. A few potted geraniums adorned its stairs, already showing signs of summer neglect. I recalled that all student houses showed signs of neglect, inside and out, year round—a preppy shabbiness eschewing materialism, a philosophical quirk of academics. Happily, most of us outgrow idealisms of youth.

"Care to take a look inside?" Kiki asked.

"No."

With a gnashing of gears and a cough from its muffler, the little car darted from the curb, and we continued on our tour. Kiki drove to the central campus and parked. We walked between two classroom buildings and emerged into the quadrangle.

Broad brick-lined walkways defined the quad's perimeter, while narrower paths crisscrossed the lawn at diagonals. Antique lampposts sprouted amid the waxy foliage of tidy fruit trees. My mind rushed with memories of the stately old buildings, the trees in spring bloom, the mobs of students darting between classes. Ambling along the now-deserted walks, our footfalls echoed in the stillness.

"Has the school grown much?" I asked Kiki.

"Hardly at all," she said. "There was talk of expansion during the late sixties when the baby-boomers were reaching college age, but it never happened. Evans has had a steady enrollment, around five thousand. The town's permanent population is still about ten thousand."

We continued to walk, exchanging bits of conversation. I learned that during Kiki's sabbatical, the theater program would be administered by Constance Garamond, who would be my "immediate supervisor." I declined Kiki's offers to tour the theater and its offices, the student union, the museum, preferring to stroll with my old friend, immersed in our youth.

"My God!" Kiki said, bringing our walk to a halt. "You must be starved. Let me show you the house and fix you lunch."

Once Kiki mentioned it, I felt famished. I'd risen much earlier than usual that day, had only coffee for breakfast, and never thought to eat on the train. I wondered if the waves of nostalgia sweeping over me were in fact only hunger pangs.

We left the quad, returning to the convertible. When I had contorted myself into my seat, Kiki revved the engine and roared off toward lunch, toward the house I had never seen, the house that would become my home.

When Kiki slowed the car and turned onto Boston Drive, I was not surprised, expecting one of the pretentious Victorians so typical of that part of town. But when Kiki pulled into her driveway, the adjacent building didn't even look like a house. It looked like a box, a three-story shoe box upended on a narrow lot, hidden from its gabled neighbors by rows of poplars. The front of the house, facing east, was entirely glass. The other three walls were towering slabs of brick. There was no front yard or garden, but a paved terrace secluded from the street by a six-foot wall. The terrace wrapped around the side of the building to a smaller box, the garage. Near it was the entrance to the house, a black door-sized plank set into the wall.

"Say something," Kiki commanded as she stopped the car on the terrace and jumped out, slinging my bag over her shoulder.

"It's not what I expected," I told her while extracting myself from the car. "When did you build it?"

"A couple of years ago. I didn't tell you about it because I didn't want you to see it until it was ready. Well," she said, flipping her hands in the air, "it's finished. Welcome to your new home. Do you like it?"

"I'm not sure yet," I answered candidly.

Kiki laughed at my skepticism as she put an arm around me and led me to the door. She swung it open and stood aside to let me pass.

I walked inside with tentative steps, then crossed to the center of the single, vast space. At the front of the room, along the bare window wall, was a low platform, a stage. Along the back wall was a row of cabinets. The middle of the room was sparsely furnished with carpeted cubes—some serving as tables, others as chairs.

The ceiling hovered three stories above. Two balconies protruded from the back wall. The lower extended halfway over the ground floor; the upper, about a third. From either, a person

might see the stage and spy on activity below. Leko spotlights and
Fresnel floods were suspended from the ceiling and from the
front edge of each loft, accessible by a metal stairway that screwed
upward through the center of the house. Rising with the stairs
was a brick column containing a fireplace at each level—a
surprisingly domestic touch.

"Approve?" Kiki asked, closing the door behind her.

No words were necessary; my smile answered.

"Wonderful," she said, clearly pleased. "How about a drink?
We'll toast our new homes and the adventures that await us." As
she spoke, she whisked across the room to the cabinets along the
back wall. She flung open several doors, revealing a fully stocked
bar and the controls for lighting and music.

"Kiki," I finally said. "You've built a little theater." I felt
instantly at home, eager to take up residence and get down to the
business of writing.

"Yes, dear, I have," she said matter-of-factly while pouring
white wine into huge balloon glasses.

"Do you ever *use* it?"

"Certainly." She handed me my glass, explaining, "I premiere
my students' experimental work in this very room. Occasionally,
visiting artists conduct master classes here. My seminars have
met here, as I suspect yours will. And—hell, Claire—it's marvelous for parties." She breathed a happy sigh and drank. "Lunch,"
she said, as though struck by a new idea. "We've got to feed you,
you poor lamb. Make yourself at home while I fix something to
eat. I'll phone Dody and Connie and ask them to come over
later."

"Hm."

"Now, now," she scolded. "No long faces. It'll be fun—we'll
call it tea or cocktails or something."

"Let's call it cocktails."

I followed Kiki up the winding stairs and discovered that the
first balcony was the kitchen. Cabinets along its back wall
matched those on the ground floor and concealed the expected
appliances. A sleek dining table sat near the front of the loft. Off
to one side were a grouping of upholstered furniture, shelving for
a wall of books, and the fireplace. "I actually 'live' up here," Kiki
told me as I looked about. "And up in the bedroom," she added,
waving toward the second loft.

While Kiki prepared lunch, I climbed the stairs to explore further. No conventional home could begin to accommodate Kiki's vast wardrobe, so the upper loft had been designed not quite as a bedroom, but as a dressing room with a bed. The bed itself was enormous, rising from the middle of the room on a platform similar to the stage downstairs. I sat on the bed and looked past the fireplace that divided the balcony's open edge. Beyond the great window, roofs and treetops tumbled down the Upper Ridge toward the silvery ribbon of Evans Run. "The view's wonderful," I called to Kiki as I wound my way down the stairs to join her in the kitchen.

I had a distinct taste for meat, but was served instead an elaborate salad composed of trendy vegetables that nice people never used to eat. I firmly believe that man cannot live on spinach greens and alfalfa sprouts alone, but I was in no position to be picky, so I consumed the mélange with coos of approval and a second glass of wine. Kiki gabbed while I ate, then excused herself to change clothes. She continued to talk from the upper loft as I forked something interesting, though tasteless, from among the garbanzos.

A shift in Kiki's tempo indicated she was no longer speaking to me, but to the bedside telephone. I resigned myself to the inevitable: Dody and Connie would soon arrive.

Within an hour, tires grated on the pebbled terrace. I abandoned my perusal of Kiki's record collection and glanced out the window. The car stopped, its doors opened, and out stepped the Evans hierarchy to examine their new charge.

"They're here," I called to Kiki, who was fussing with the final touches of another change of clothes.

"I'll be right down."

As she spoke, the visitors knocked. I crossed to the door and opened it.

"Good afternoon," I said brightly. It was nearly six o'clock, but "evening" can imply dinner, and I intended to limit the encounter to a quick drink. "Do come in," I continued, more as a command than a welcome. "Kiki will be with us shortly. I'm Claire Gray."

"Of course, Miss Gray," the white-haired man bubbled. "As if introductions were necessary!" He pumped my hand.

I waited. Since introductions were in fact necessary, I was

tempted to ask, And who are you?

"I'm Connie Garamond, English department," the woman said, rescuing the conversation with a smile. She extended her hand, and I shook it, deciding at once that I liked her.

"And I . . . ," said the man, clearing his throat as a sort of fanfare, "I am Doddson Clark Henry."

There was a pregnant pause.

Connie explained, "Dody is president of Evans College."

"I see." I said the words through a slim, disinterested smile. "So pleased to meet you, Mr. Henry." I deliberately did not address him as President or Professor, hoping he would be irked by my civilian attitude.

I ushered the guests away from the door, toward the bar at the back of the room. "Now, what can I get you?" I asked, assuming the role of hostess in my home-to-be. "Tonic perhaps? Nothing like a tonic to cool a warm afternoon."

"My yes, indeed," Dody agreed. "Gin and tonic, but make it a light one, please."

"Certainly, Mr. Henry. And you, Connie?"

"Straight vodka on the rocks, please. With a twist."

"Sure," I told her with a satisfied nod. She had confirmed her likability—the woman knew how to drink.

Going to work at the bar, I watched the guests with sidelong glances as they browsed about the room. Doddson Clark Henry struck me as a fidgeting weasel, about retirement age. On that July afternoon he wore a black three-piece suit that made him look statesmanlike, stiff, dead. His gaze shifted furtively, betraying disdain for Kiki's newfangled living room.

Constance Garamond was more nearly my own age, perhaps in her late forties. I had expected the English department chair to be a matronly frump whose sole titillation sprang from dog-eared passages of Chaucer. I found her instead to be quick-witted and worldly. She wore sandals, tasteful slacks, and a loose summer blouse. She laughed quietly when Dody asked her something about the stage in front of the window.

I poured Connie's vodka and mixed myself a kir. On a devilish impulse, I prepared Dody's "light" gin and tonic with a half tumbler of gin and a delicate splash of mix. While garnishing the glasses, I asked my guests to be seated. Connie chose a carpeted cube beneath the edge of the balcony. Dody perched on the cube next to hers. Glancing warily at a spotlight suspended overhead, he moved to another cube, out of the path of the fixture, should it fall.

"Here we are," I said cheerily, distributing the glasses. I raised my own in a toast. "To the coming school year."

"To the success of your play," Connie offered.

"My yes, indeed," chimed Dody.

We all drank.

"Drinks okay?" I asked with perfect composure, watching Dody as the gin rolled past his tongue. "Good," I said, having heard no complaints. Dody, of course, was unable to complain, still struggling to swallow.

"I see you've all gotten down to business," said Kiki, announcing her arrival at the top of the stairs. She was dressed in a sequined gown of emerald green, the sort of dress that might appear on a Viennese balcony against a backdrop of blazing chandeliers. A clump of peacock feathers sprayed from her hair. Having captured the silent gaze of her audience, she babbled effusively while swirling down the stairs.

"I assume you've all met—what a clumsy hostess I am! Claire, do meet Doddson Clark Henry, president of our hallowed halls. Everyone calls him Dody. You really must. And wait till you meet Dody's wife, Camille. You'll simply love the woman. Connie here is your supervisor, your *boss*, Claire, and I must caution you: She really cracks her whip. Just kidding, darling, of course. And the sooner you meet Connie's husband, Paul, the better. He's such a charmer. Oh God, we simply *must* have a party—a big party. Dody, weren't you planning a reception in honor of Claire's arrival next month?"

Kiki delivered the question over her shoulder as she crossed to the bar to mix her own drink.

"My yes, indeed—Camille and I were discussing the reception this afternoon."

I raised my brows, feigning interest, while a knot in my stomach discharged something distinctly acidic.

"We were thinking," Dody continued, one finger poised in the air, "that the first Saturday in August, your first weekend in Evanstown, would be a perfect evening. Everyone could meet you—if you'd be available, Miss Gray."

"I'd be delighted," I lied through a smile.

"Wonderful!" Kiki gushed while swooping with her drink to pose behind Dody and Connie. "You'll soon see, Claire darling, what you've been missing here at Evans all these years. I can't wait till you meet the rest of our happy little family."

Looking upon Kiki Jasper-Plunkett's happy little family, I was struck by the strange tableau they presented. Their costumes, their esoteric pursuits, even their unlikely names. And there I sat: Claire Gray. Suddenly I saw them as characters in a play, as actors rehearsing. I sipped my kir while Kiki jabbered gaily.

I wonder now where George was that day. Was he near? Did our paths cross that afternoon?

Too quickly, it was the last Saturday of July, nine o'clock, the night of Hector's party. I sat at my dressing table looking into the mirror. Closet doors gaped behind me; cartons were stacked everywhere. Packing for a move is an uprooting exercise, rife with the uncertainties of change, but once the cartons are sealed and the grime of the years has been cleaned from under the bed, then it's time to go. I was ready.

In a few days I would make my move to Evanstown. In a week I would groom myself for Dody and Camille's reception. But that night at my dressing table, I groomed for Hector Bosch, for Arnold Manley, for the New York theater crowd that was gathering to say good-bye. My hair looked fine. Eyes too. And I had a red dress on.

I love red—bloody, virile, scarlet red. I don't wear it often, but there are times when it seems distinctly apropos. Parties, of course. Openings of plays. And any occasion that hints of sex. Were I to marry, I would wear a red wedding gown—not only for the honesty of the statement, but for the punch, the touch of pizazz it would lend to the event.

Though I pride myself on being punctual, when Hector says nine, he means ten. So I winked at myself and raised the glass of kir that sat on the dressing table. My companion in the mirror did likewise. We drank.

"Evening, Miss Gray," said Hector's doorman with a toothy smile. It was ten o'clock. "Want to wish you best of luck next year, case I'm off duty when you folks finish up."

"Thank you, dear. Things starting to roll up there?"

"Yes, *ma'am*," he assured me, escorting me into the lobby.

The elevator rose forty floors above Manhattan. When its doors slid open, laughter and music drew me down the hall toward Hector's apartment. Aware of my heartbeat, my rising pulse, I felt the same sensation known to any actor listening for his cue to walk onstage. With a surge of adrenaline, I made my entrance.

"She's here, everybody!" someone shouted above the din.

Voices and music fell silent. Heads turned. Like Moses surveying the Red Sea, I gazed from the doorway upon the crowd before me, a crowd that parted to let me pass, closing quickly behind. Familiar faces greeted me as I crossed the room—hellos, best wishes, good-byes—clasp of the hand, kiss on the cheek.

The party grew raucous again by the time I reached Hector. He wore formal evening attire, impeccably black and white, with the tiniest red rosebud adorning his lapel. Before an expansive wall of glass, he leaned in the crook of a grand piano. Its lacquered ebony mirrored the lights of the city below while a pianist banged out stylish show tunes, unnoticed by the yattering, laughing crowd. Easily a hundred people were there, and the night, as they say, was young.

"Good evening, my dear," said Hector as he leaned forward with a kiss. "So glad you dropped by."

"Everything's lovely," I told him. "I'm overwhelmed."

"We could entertain this way every weekend, my darling, if you'd forget this college nonsense and be my bride."

"Could I wear red lace?"

"Certainly," he said at once, calling my bluff. "How about it?"

"No, Hector."

He shrugged his shoulders, sighed wistfully, then instructed a girl in a kimono to bring me a kir from the bar at the far side of the room.

The vast apartment occupied most of the building's fortieth floor. Suffice it to say, Hector's theatrical flair was reflected in the decoration of his home. Each time I visited, the apartment was redone in a radical new style. I could never resist razzing him for this extravagance. "Well, Hector, I see you've pulled another Auntie Mame."

"I beg your pardon?" he asked innocently, pretending not to catch the allusion.

I answered, "Nice gong," jerking my head toward the enormous circle of brass that hung from the ceiling near the piano. The apartment now sported an Oriental look.

The girl in the kimono (one of several, I now noticed) returned with my drink on a tray. She and Hector bowed from the waist to each other.

He handed me the glass, saying, "I'm so glad you approve. The gong, however, is not merely decorative." His tone was now coy. "Its exotic charms aside, this instrument was installed tonight for a baldly utilitarian purpose—the purpose of making an announcement that the Broadway hoi polloi have expected for years. The announcement of our intended nuptials."

I choked on my kir and slipped into an indelicate seizure of coughing.

Hector grinned. He reached for the huge padded mallet, took aim, and whacked the gong deftly with a magnificent, reverberating blow.

Several guests standing near us dropped their glasses. The pianist stumbled on a final, unwritten chord. Conversations were nipped midsentence as all faces turned to Hector, unsure if the disturbance was meant to provoke laughter or demand silence. Silence finally prevailed, broken only by my spasm of coughs. My eyes were inflamed and tear-filled; anyone who noticed would presume I was crying.

"Ladies and gentlemen, my dear friends," Hector began in his orator's tone, "I apologize for the disturbance of your merrymaking, but I have a sterling little nugget of information that I am sure will interest all present. Yes, gentle friends, I have an announcement regarding the future plans of the charming and talented Claire Gray and myself."

I turned from the crowd and peered out the window, weighing the prospect of a forty-floor leap.

Hector beamed slyly at his audience. He waited while ripples of conversation lapsed to silence, then his smile gave way to laughter. Through rude guffaws, he finally announced, "The wedding . . . the wedding's off."

"What wedding?" I asked in mock horror as the crowd erupted with boos and catcalls.

"Hector Bosch has spoken?" someone asked over the din.

"No," I retorted before Hector could answer, "*I've* spoken."

There was laughter from the crowd as the party took off with renewed vigor. Hector summoned the kimono girls, ordering drinks for the guests who'd dropped their glasses. The pianist decided to take a break, so he switched on the stereo, playing something loud and primal. People began dancing wherever they could find a bare patch of floor. I also danced—quite well, too, if my judgment can be trusted.

Around eleven, when the shows let out, a fresh influx of guests arrived, including Arnold Manley. As the second guest of honor, he was greeted with a round of applause. When he'd made his way through the crowd to where I stood, we embraced for a long moment, then kissed. It was not a sensual kiss, but an expression of mutual triumph between mentor and protégé.

"I'll miss you, Claire."

"Likewise, kiddo. Time to grow a little, right? We'd suffocate if we never took a chance, never faced a risk. I'm counting on you, Manny. Go to Hollywood, wow 'em with *Inner Moments*, then come home and do it again with *Traders*."

"It's a deal."

We shook hands. To be certain our pact was ironclad, we joined each other in a drink, the first of many that evening, toasting the ventures that lay ahead.

Feeling their cocktails, several guests were lured to give Hector's gong an experimental wallop. When the clamor became more annoying than amusing, Hector moved his toy out of the living room and into a distant bedroom. As the night wore on, bursts of muted thunder wafted repeatedly through the apartment. God only knows what antics prompted the banging of the gong—though one may guess.

While Hector's parties are always triumphs, that one topped them all. As Hector himself might proclaim, it was a smash of a bash. I was by no means the last to leave, and it was dawn before I said my farewells.

People seem surprised to see me enjoy myself. Maybe they think I'm too sophisticated to have fun. That's odd. Parties are so uplifting, with such remarkable curative powers.

George understood that. I wish he could have been there, my last weekend in New York. He'd have loved Hector's party.

PART TWO
BASTARD AMBER

G E O R G E

Christ, I hate faculty parties. A bunch of stuffed shirts get together to guzzle jug wine from plastic glasses, trying to impress each other's spouses with the buzzwords of their "disciplines."

"George, my good man! Great to see you again. Guy should bring you to more of our little gatherings."

I smile, jerking a nod of agreement while the old gasbag slaps my back with forced chumminess. He tells me to have fun. Sure. I smile again over the rim of the glass, which sticks to my lower lip. A slug of the cheap Chablis rushes past my tongue, down my throat. It is too sweet, too warm. Its musky taste matches its smell.

These evenings are not without reward, though. I'm usually the center of attention, like an exotic animal paraded on a leash for the amusement of genteel, more conventional folk. But tonight is different. I'm here, like all the others, to meet Claire

Gray. She should arrive any moment.

I am an actor, a damned good amateur who ought to be a pro. But opportunity rarely knocks in a burg like Evanstown. Sure, I could pack my bags and move to New York. Why not? Because Broadway is the most competitive market in the world, a buyer's market that I would enter as a seller of myself. Poised at the brink of middle age, secure in my other job, I'm shrewd enough to recognize that a successful acting career isn't built merely on talent or ambition. Success is a blessing that is bestowed by others—the contacts, the friends, the people you know. People like Claire Gray.

I've known a few women directors, all bitches. The ones I've worked with were impossible. I wonder if Claire Gray fits the mold. I do know this: She's the best, and she's come to Evanstown. She'll write a play this year and direct it in the spring. I plan to be in it. I want the leading role.

So this is not a typical faculty party. It's a reception at the home of the college president, Doddson Clark Henry. Dody mingles with his guests like a stranger in his own living room. They yammer the jargon of higher learning, slurping their wine against the drone of nonstop Vivaldi. Though it's August, they dress as in the dead of winter, for the closets of the halls of ivy are stuffed not only with dark secrets of conceit and frustration, but with serviceable, "intelligent" classroom wardrobes. The gentlemen are wearing their tweeds and elbow patches; many of the ladies are too.

Dody and his wife are conspicuous exceptions. Dody, as always, wears a black suit. Camille Henry, the first lady of Evans College, is sheathed from neck to ankles in velvet and ruffles. I can't imagine these two in bed.

I'm the other exception, wearing not tweeds, but tight, dressy jeans and a tighter knit shirt. Proper for August, proper for a party. And proper for a man with my body, a body I'm not ashamed to display.

I know everyone in the room. This is a small town, and we all know each other, but only Kiki Jasper-Plunkett knows Claire Gray. They went to school here together. Kiki isn't here yet, and I presume she will deliver the guest of honor. So where are they?

The room is charged with anticipation. The music seems louder. Conversations are less intellectual now, edged with giddy, pointless laughter. Dody stalks the room, smiling cautiously at his guests, offering more wine. Camille is fixed dutifully near the front door to greet new arrivals, fluttering her hands in animated discussion with a coven of faculty wives. She never meanders more than a few tiny steps, returning to the door as if tethered to the knob. And I stand alone, immersed in this inner monologue, sipping from the plastic glass, finding that the wine tastes better now.

There is a knock at the door. Kiki enters with Claire Gray and introduces her to Camille and the ladies nearby. As Kiki and her friend make their way into the living room, the wives at the door compare notes in breathy whispers. Word quickly spreads that *she* is here, but these sophisticated bastards hide their excitement by plodding deeper into their pompous dialogues, acting surprised when Dody ushers her forward. Awed by her presence, I stand staring.

Claire Gray is fifty or so, the same age as Kiki. She is a striking woman, not beautiful, but stylish and self-confident. If she feels uncomfortable among these alien creatures, she doesn't show it. She's in control.

You can't miss her. She's wearing tailored linen slacks and a sweeping silk tunic of vivid scarlet, unbuttoned to midchest to reveal a glimpse of cleavage. A long gold chain slinks in and out of the blouse with the rhythm of her speech, clicking past the unfastened buttons as she tosses her head with an occasional laugh. Once in New York, I thought I spotted Claire Gray in the audience at one of her plays. She wore red. This is the same woman.

She is talking with a group of faculty clustered near me. They wear polite smiles while nodding at her words, feeding her their questions, exposing the nonsense that can flower only in the hothouse of academia. She answers with candid humor and a hint of condescension. I sip my Chablis, openly eavesdropping.

"Don't you agree, Miss Gray, that scholastic theater programs, a source of artistic enrichment for student audiences, also provide young actors and actresses with a valuable outlet for the exploration and ultimate discovery of the self?" The man speaking teaches history of theater, and his interest in drama is purely literary. Once, many years ago, he directed a production. He has never been invited to repeat the effort.

Claire Gray has listened soberly and now pauses to consider her answer. Grinning, she begins to speak. "I agree, professor, that academic theater serves these purposes. But to reduce playmaking to its instructive or therapeutic uses is a grave injustice to the art—for theater is an art, an ancient art that man has employed through the ages to breathe life into his loftiest thoughts, his basest desires, his most profound dilemmas. Man takes to the stage to give his audience a glimpse of what was or what might be, for better or worse. Ideas and values are freely traded. The actor has an ability to entertain. He trades it for the applause and dollars of his audience. Work is traded for laughter or tears. Inspiration is traded for ego. This is the essence of theater. It's the nature of art. And what's truly remarkable about this exchange, gentlemen, is that when the curtain falls, when actors and audience have given from the depths of their minds and emotions, everyone has become richer. Isn't that amazing?"

Her question is met with stunned silence. Vacant stares reveal the confused panic of intellectuals who fear they have met their match. She looks from face to face.

Paul Garamond is among the listeners. "It seems," he finally says, "that the paradigmatic basis of your theory, Miss Gray, springs from a philosophical construct that differs rather markedly from the fundamental tenets of our own model."

"You mean you disagree," she blurts with a laugh that couldn't give a damn, further unsettling her listeners.

"Miss Gray," continues Garamond, "disagreement is such a divisive wedge. Academic society, after all, is held together by a delicate network of minds. Differing intellectual stances do, however, provide the very fodder of growth. I am certain, ergo, that I speak for the entire faculty, Miss Gray, when I bid you welcome. Let us forge ahead, committed to this rare opportunity to explore each other's views."

"My yes, indeed!" chirps Dody, clasping his hands together with a child's enthusiasm.

Claire Gray eyes her new co-workers warily. She smiles, emitting only a "Hm."

I've inched my way forward and at last take my cue to speak. "Miss Gray, have you met Paul Garamond?"

She glances first at me, then studies Garamond. "No, I haven't. Pleased to meet you, Paul. I've met your wife. Charming woman." She explains to the group, "Connie's my boss."

"Mine too," says Garamond, and everyone laughs.

A round of introductions follows. Garamond finally returns my courtesy, almost as an afterthought. "And this, Miss Gray," he motions toward me, "this is George McBeth."

She shakes my hand, asking, "Macbeth? Like the play?"

"It's McBeth," I tell her, stressing the difference.

"Risky theater name, even so. Are you on the faculty?"

"I do act, Miss Gray, but no, I don't teach."

"I thought not." Her tone is approving. She winks.

"And you, Paul?" she asks. "I know you're on the faculty, but what do you teach?"

"Writing. I'm in the English department, but my true love is theater. I consider myself something of a playwright, albeit an amateur."

"Amateur? Nonsense!" pipes in Dody, anxious to pump up the esteem of his faculty. "I assure you, Miss Gray, that Paul Garamond is no dilettante. Why, just this summer, one of his works was produced Off Broadway."

"It was nothing," Garamond assures us in a modest tone unnatural to him. "It was an experimental piece, by no means fully developed."

His speech is tinged with nervousness, an air of apology—and I think I know why. Noticing that Claire Gray's glass is empty, I offer to be of service. "Can I get you more wine, Miss Gray."

"I'd love some. In fact, I'll go with you. Excuse me, gentlemen."

As I escort her away from the group, glances follow us across the room. Whispered gossip is lost beneath the babble and the Vivaldi. Arriving at the dining room buffet, which has been set up as a bar, I refill her glass, then mine.

"Thank you, Mr. McBeth."

"Please call me George."

"Thank you, George. And you must call me Claire."

I hide my satisfaction behind a slurp of wine. I don't believe this: I'm standing here drinking with Broadway's finest director, already on a first-name basis. I wonder how I'm doing. Is my hair okay? Are my ambitions showing?

"You're an actor," she says, eyeing me.

Uncertain of her meaning, I don't respond.

She explains, "You said that you act but don't teach. Have you done many plays?"

"Yes, Claire, I have. I'm involved with the Evanstown Players. We're an amateur group, but a good one. We perform in our own playhouse, and many of us appear in the college productions as well."

"Any leads?"

"I usually play leading roles."

A smile flashes past her face. I expect her to say, I thought so. But she doesn't need to.

As we begin to get acquainted, our conversation becomes more comfortable, quicker, turning freely as we explore each other's worlds. She learns that I am soon to turn forty (I don't look it and don't like it), that I was divorced many years ago and now live with a younger man, Guy Anderson, who is on the English faculty. I am a decorator—"a living cliché," I tell her—employed by a furniture store, Potter's, the only prestige shop in the area. I hate my job and dislike my boss, but love to act. Evanstown frustrates me, and I make it obvious to Claire that I would gladly move on.

She reveals nothing about herself that I don't already know. She mentions her school days at Evans, her friendship with Kiki, her plans to write a play. But I'm well aware of these details. Claire Gray has been studied from afar.

When I mention what a thrill it is to meet her, she sidesteps my flattery, switching to the topic of her new co-workers. High on her list of concerns are Dody and Connie, the only two people at Evans who will outrank Claire.

I assure her that Doddson Henry is more intimidated by her than she need be by him. "His sole presidential quality is his pomposity. Connie Garamond, of course, is another matter. She's dedicated to her work; she's able and talented. You'll find it a pleasure to work with her."

"I met Connie a few weeks ago and liked her at once. But what about Paul? He's not at all what I expected."

I laugh in agreement. "Yes, I'd say Connie made a distinct error of judgment on that one. I don't know what she sees in him. Maybe she married him for his name. 'Garamond' sounds fabulous for a woman of letters."

"Hm. Does it?" She thinks for a moment before asking

bluntly, "Is McBeth your real name?"

I smile, but I don't answer.

"Anyway," she continues, "what was that business about Paul's play? He seemed . . . embarrassed by it."

"He should be." I'm grinning shamelessly. "It must have been God-awful. All I know is that he called it *Broken Toys.*"

"*Broken Toys?* I saw that play, the worst in years! How does he muster the nerve to show his face after such a fiasco? Hector Bosch devoted a column to it, the same one that announced I'd be coming to Evanstown. Didn't you see it?"

"No, Claire. None of us saw it."

"Good God," she says with a start, covering her mouth with her fingers. "I'd forgotten. Kiki told me. The papers disappeared—as if they'd been stolen."

"It's plain enough who did it. Since that little incident, Guy and I have had the *Review* delivered to our home."

It is Paul himself who interrupts us, stepping forward to refill his glass. "Miss Gray," he says while pouring some wine, "I'd like you to meet Doctor Solomon and his . . . uh, his friend, Nigel Slough."

Claire shakes hands with the two men, exchanging the usual pleasantries, then asks, "What do you teach, Doctor Solomon?"

"I don't teach, Miss Gray. I'm a medical doctor."

I explain, "Doctor Solomon is a psychiatrist. Nigel, a grad student, is his lover."

Paul reacts to my words squeamishly, but Solomon and Nigel aren't fazed, and Claire seems relieved that we needn't play games.

"A psychiatrist?" she says with raised brows. "I'm surprised your services would be needed in Evanstown."

"Business is brisk," he assures her.

"I'm one of Doc Solomon's better customers," I tell the group. "It's comforting to know *someone* in town who has his head together."

This comment draws a sarcastic sniff from Nigel Slough, who hasn't spoken since being introduced. He is several years younger than anyone else in the room and unquestionably attractive, though in a petulant, pretty sort of way. Solomon responds to his lover's condescension with a perturbed sigh.

Claire asks Nigel, "What do you study, Mr. Slough?"

"Economics. I've completed my courses and shall begin the dissertation phase this year. I have tentatively entitled my thesis *The Homoerotic Basis of Capitalism.*"

Stunned but undaunted, she responds, "How intriguing. I always presumed the basis of capitalism to be profit."

"No no no," he clucks, as if correcting a naive child. "Consider the French Revolution."

"Yes?"

"By deposing monarchical rule, the French people embraced capitalism as an economic system that would not only provide a framework for commerce and finance, but would shape an entirely new worldview for all strata of their society—a worldview characterized by greed, materialism, and self-interest. It's instructive to note the intellectual climate in which the Revolution was born. The illuminati of the late Eighteenth Century were known as much for their sexual aberration as for their creative thinking. The Marquis de Sade, for example, immediately predates the Revolution. So the overthrow provides us with a cosmographic model of the Freudian paradigm, leaving us with an intractable lesson: The rebellion was mere ritual. But the ritual carried immense meaning. Today there is no ritual, so there can be no meaning."

Nigel is clearly proud of himself for having pieced together this garbage. He grins, awaiting our bravos, but his sole reward is Claire's noncommittal "Hm."

"Shall I explain further?" he finally asks.

"No, thank you, Mr. Slough. I'll catch it in paperback."

There is laughter all around. Nigel, usually too quick to find himself the brunt of a joke, looks pale. In mock consolation I tell him, "I don't know if you're right or wrong. That stuff's way over my head. But the title's terrific."

"Titles *are* interesting," notes Solomon. "I'm sure they carry clues to the psychological makeup of their authors. Does an author, for example, go about naming a book or a play in the same way he would name a baby? Both processes—writing and procreation—are essentially the same creative act."

"They are?" Claire asks, suppressing a laugh.

"Yes, Miss Gray, I think all creativity stems from the same human drive. For instance," he turns to Garamond, "you, Paul, had a play on Broadway."

"Off Broadway."

"I forget now—what did you call it?"

"It was a very short run, a mere exercise."

Claire asks innocently, "Wasn't it called *Broken Toys?*"

"Ah, that's it," Solomon continues, "*Broken Toys*. While I don't even know what the play was about, it doesn't take an analyst to guess deeper meanings embedded in such a title. Would the author care to enlighten us?"

"No, actually, I wouldn't," says Paul through a nervous smile. "You see, that play's behind me now, and I'm busily at work on a new one. Returning to analyze *Broken Toys* might hinder my creative flow."

I ask, "What's the name of your new play?"

"Now *that's* another matter," he says with a sparkle in his eye, eager to discuss what he hasn't yet written. "My next play shall be known as *Magnum Opus.*"

Doctor Solomon breaks our embarrassed silence with a cough, then says, "Well, there's not much point in analyzing a work in progress, is there?"

"No," agrees his lover, Nigel, "but I'm curious. Miss Gray, you're here to write a play, aren't you? Do you have a working title?"

"Indeed I do," she tells him. "I'm calling it *Traders.*"

"Oh? It sounds like an economic treatise. Is it?"

"Partly, I suppose."

"Please, tell me more."

"I'm afraid you wouldn't understand, Mr. Slough."

Spent shampoo slides down my body like fingers of white mud. Needles of water prick my skin. Feels good. I can think here. The hiss of the shower wraps me in its tiled womb.

Thinking out loud sometimes. Talking to myself, touching myself. But not now. Sorting through the options, making plans. Rehearsing.

Remembering last night, the party for Claire Gray. I met her, gained her confidence. She liked me, asked about my acting. I told her of my many leading roles. "I thought so," she said. Doesn't seem real.

"Can't be real," thinking out loud, touching myself. But not

now. Remembering last night, after the party, home again with
Guy. In bed with him, talking with the lights out, balancing a
drink on my chest—a real drink, sick of the wine, trying to wash
its taste from my mouth.

"Stop chewing ice," Guy said. "It sounds awful, and it'll wreck
your teeth. Besides, you know what they say about ice-chompers,
their frustrations and anxieties . . . "

"I already have a shrink, thank you. And believe me, one's
enough."

"Tell me about it—I pay the bills."

"Look, Guy. I can't afford him on my own."

"I know that," he told me, rolling over to rest his head on my
shoulder. "Professors earn more than decorators, at least in this
town, so I *can* afford it. Relax. You seem tense."

"Just excited. My God, I met Claire Gray tonight. Wasn't she
fabulous?"

"How would I know? I never got to meet her. You had her
cornered all evening."

"We had a lot to talk about. We have a lot in common.
'Theater is my life,' she told me. It's my life, too."

"What about Potter's? I thought decorating was your life."

"Don't remind me." Perturbed by the thought of my job, I
drained my glass and sucked a piece of ice into my mouth.
Cracking it between my molars, I swallowed half.

"Stop that. And you'd better not tell Neil, 'Theater is my life.'
That's not why he pays you."

"Neil? You mean Nellie Potter, that dizzy old queen?"

"What are you bitching about? He's always been good to you.
He keeps you in designer jeans."

I snorted a lascivious laugh. "If he had his way, he'd get me
out of my jeans." I wagged my limp cock at Guy, in case he missed
the point.

"Who wouldn't, slugger? He wouldn't be the first."

"Or the last," I assured him.

"So? As long as you're giving it away, you might as well give
it to someone who can do you some good. Give the old man a
thrill. Maybe there'd be a promotion in it."

Guy was joking, but I gathered my thoughts before answering.
"Don't you understand?" I said slowly. "Nellie can't do a thing
for me. I have no ambitions as a decorator."

"It's what you do best."

"*Acting* is what I do best."

"Okay, okay. But have you considered combining your talents in theater and decorating? How about set design?"

"That's for sissies."

"Bear in mind, cupcake, that you qualify."

"Cunt." Having closed the topic of my career, I returned to the more crucial business of chewing ice.

But Guy persisted. "Remember when you buried Butch under the birdbath? It was a spectacle. Everyone said so. And you had a ball decorating the garden. It was a real fairyland, if you'll pardon the expression. The event was pure theater. You could do it, George."

"Get serious. It was a funeral for a weimaraner, a dog's burial. While it was a lovely garden party, the fact remains that decorating—sets or otherwise—is not my calling. Acting is."

"Yeah? What are you going to do about it?" he asked point-blank.

"There's always Claire Gray."

"What does that mean?"

I explained, "She's here to write a play. I want the leading role. I might have to fuck her for it, but I plan to get the part."

"I'm the first to admit, George, that your talents in the boudoir are extraordinary, but she might be more interested in your talents onstage."

"That was tacky."

"No tackier than the thought of bedding Claire Gray. Nothing personal against the woman, but she's old enough to be your mother."

"*Your* mother, Guy. You're thirty, I'm forty, she's fifty—roughly—so she's no older to me than I am to you. Do I detect a note of jealousy?"

"I know you whore around," he answered without hesitation. "When you trick with a man, of course I'm jealous—not because you've been unfaithful, but because I didn't get to him first. This is different, though. If you suddenly want to get involved with a woman, for whatever reason, be my guest. Just keep in mind that it's a dangerous game, screwing around with your . . . identity. You won't enjoy it. I doubt if you even know how."

"Aren't we forgetting my wife and daughter?"

"Your ex-wife," he reminded me. "And as for the girl, you haven't seen her since her fifth birthday. That was over ten years ago, long before I met you. I don't even know their names, for God's sake—a pretty good gauge of how you relish the memory of your 'straight experience.'"

"Things were different then," I told him calmly. "The climate toward gays wasn't exactly warm and accepting, you know. It was downright hostile. I did what I had to do. Yes, the marriage was a disaster. No, the baby couldn't save it. Melodrama, tears, cliché ending. You were lucky, Guy. Not morally superior, just historically lucky. Things changed between my coming-out and yours. Not much, but enough to make a difference."

"That's my point, George. If your sexual identity was arrived at so painfully, why risk a mindbender with Claire Gray for a part in a school play? Seems like a pretty stiff price."

"Speaking of stiff . . . ," I said in a different, suggestive tone, referring to my erection. I watched with satisfaction as it bobbed toward the ceiling.

"I noticed. Very nice," he said, sounding bored. "Now I'm not trying to compliment you . . . "

"God forbid."

". . . but you're the best actor in town, and everyone knows it. Sidestep the casting couch and try out for the role like anyone else. You'll get it."

"Maybe. Probably. But I have to make sure. There's more at stake than a part in a play." I began to masturbate with an easy, comfortable stroke.

"What's at stake? Your ego?"

"Sure. But it goes beyond that. Hard to explain."

Of course I couldn't explain. How could I tell him what was really on my mind? How could I share the dream that will take me away, leaving him behind?

Our conversation lapsed. He was tired, but I was exhilarated. With one arm I cradled Guy's shoulders; with the other I still stroked myself. In the dark silence, I turned my face toward his and kissed him.

"Come on," I whispered, hoping to spark his interest.

He broke the tender moment with a terse laugh. "Better save it, George," he said while rolling over, turning his back to me. "You'll need it later."

I grunted as if to say, Have it your way, baby, I'll handle this myself. I tried beating off in earnest, but my mind was filled with other thoughts, and my grip became painful. Guy was right—I'd better save it.

Rolling toward him on my side, I nestled against his back, draped an arm around his chest, and tried to sleep. But I was wide awake, wired with excitement. Fitfully, I rearranged myself on the bed and listened to the ringing in my ears.

Sleep came very late, induced at last by sheer exhaustion. When I awoke midmorning, Guy wasn't there. I thought he'd gone to class, and I felt the momentary panic of being late for work. But it was Sunday.

I tossed back the sheet and stretched lazily, eyeing the erection that failed me last night but returned, as it does most mornings, to greet me. Bottled up, overdue, I was tempted to take care of it there in bed—but no. Better save it. Maybe in the shower.

After long, uncounted minutes under the spray, my mind is now cleansed of its night-grogginess, my body goaded back to life. Hot drops bite my skin. I stand motionless, remembering last night. Talking to myself, touching myself.

"Better save it," thinking out loud, thinking of Claire, New York, and beyond. I again feel the exhilaration of last night, again take hold of myself. "Better save it."

Not convinced, I begin to pull. Won't take long, waiting for it. Remembering Guy, the triumphs of our bed. Thoughts grow shorter as my hand pumps harder. Fleeting images, rapid-fire. Pictures, not words. Sounds and smells.

Legs. Games. Points of view. Unplanned contortions, unrepeatable, nameless. Remembering all of it, real and unreal. Play of water on my tongue. Not hearing the spray, only the sliding of my hand, amplified and focused, faster and louder. With mind and fingers I probe my body—countless little probings, both gentle and violent—which at last flicks the switch and there's no turning back. Won't take long. Thinking of Guy, finding the rhythm, scratching his shoulders. Hate to leave him. "Hate to lose you." How long, a year? Any moment.

My back arches with an electric rush from brain to groin. Squatting, panting, working hard. Swallowing water. "Oh God," I gasp, oh Guy. It clouds my senses, grips me, purges me in long, repeated streaks.

I've staggered back to brace myself against the wet tile wall, waiting for oblivion to pass, catching my breath, watching my orgasm slip down the drain like stringy raw egg white.

"Better save it," I remind myself. I'll need it later.

Saturday night, September already, a month since I met her. Claire Gray is coming to the house for dinner. After seven already, and still a million things to do.

"Slow down," Guy tells me, "or you'll be smashed before she gets here." He steps behind me at the kitchen counter, hugs my waist, and kisses the nape of my neck.

"How do I get into these things?"

"You invited her," he reminds me. "What's the problem? Table's set, flowers are fabulous, meat's ready to grill."

"The salad. You know I'm a wreck till the damn salad's under control. Here," I tell him, sliding mustard, olive oil, and vinegar across the counter. "Do your vinaigrette."

Without a word, he grabs a wire whisk and sets to work on the dressing. Relieved of this chore, I pour another drink. Guy flashes me a disdainful glance.

"Don't worry," I tell him, "I won't get smashed. This casual little supper has to be perfect."

"It'll be perfect, but it won't be casual. The only thing casual about this 'little supper' is your jeans."

"It's a studied look, an intended contrast. There's something nicely decadent about the mixture of sterling, Lalique, and black denim. Besides, I look good in jeans."

"Besides, you can show off your crotch better."

"Doesn't hurt," I admit with a broad smile.

"You *are* a whore."

I raise my glass in agreement. Surveying the kitchen and glancing into the dining room, I decide that Guy is right—everything's under control. I check my watch. Nothing to do now but wait.

I wonder if she'll be on time, what she'll wear, what the evening might hold. I silently rehearse greeting her. How familiar should I act? We've met only twice.

At Dody and Camille's party last month, I met Claire and made her aware of me, but that doesn't cinch a part in her play, and it certainly doesn't get me to New York. So I worked up the courage to visit her at home last week. The house belongs to Kiki Jasper-Plunkett, but she's in New York for the year. I've seen it from the street many times—everyone in town has driven by to gawk—but I'd never been inside.

I went there one afternoon on my way home from work. I parked on the street and walked through a walled courtyard to an imposing black door. I knocked and waited, and knocked again. I was about to turn and leave when the door finally swung open and Claire peered out at me.

"Oh," she said pleasantly, "Mr. McBeth, isn't it?"

"George," I reminded her.

"Of course, do come in," she said in a hurried voice. "I was on the phone. Still am. Will you excuse me?"

She went to a telephone at the far corner of the room, leaving me free to explore. I ambled about with my hands in my pockets, gazing like a tourist at the two balconies, the theatrical lighting, and the ceiling three stories above. Along the front wall, beneath a single huge window, was a stage. I sat on its edge, clasping a knee with both hands. While studying the room, I listened to Claire on the phone. She was talking to someone named Manny. They spoke of California and New York, mentioning "the script," "the shooting," and assorted last names.

Manny, I wondered—Jewish? Maybe an agent.

"Do keep me posted, Manny. I'll do the same. Kisses, darling." And she hung up the phone.

I love the way she calls everyone "darling" or "dear," not like Tallulah or the Gabors, not affectedly. It's a sweet little greeting to let you know she won't bite.

"Sorry to keep you waiting, George. Can I get you anything?" she offered, sweeping her hand across a row of cupboards, presumably the bar.

"No, thanks," I said, rising from the edge of the stage. "I can't stay long. I hope you don't mind uninvited guests."

"Not at all. Small towns are supposed to be neighborly." She studied my gaze and laughed. "Haven't you been here before?"

"Not inside," I told her, also laughing. "I'd heard about it, but I wasn't prepared for *this*." I waved my arms in a gesture that took in the entire house.

"You're a decorator, aren't you? I should think you'd find this sort of place old hat."

"Not in Evanstown. This style is known in the trade as 'minimal.' They're not ready for it here. Too severe."

"I'd call it 'urban.' Suffice it to say, this sort of living is an acquired taste, but then, don't you sometimes get the itch to branch out and expand your repertoire?"

"Sure," I conceded at once. "I've been meaning to urbanize my life. I could start at home. Slick it up. Guy often kids me about how I've decorated our place. It's so 'pretty,' he says, it looks as if a couple of old ladies live there. You should see it."

"I'd love to."

I eyed her with a meaningful "Aha!" and explained, "That's why I'm here. Guy and I would like to invite you to dinner at our home next Saturday. We know it's short notice, but hope you can make it."

"I'd be delighted. Everyone in town must assume my life's a social whirl, booked solid. I'm dying to get out, but no one invites me. I think they're all afraid of me."

"I'm not afraid of you."

"I know you're not, dear," she said with a smile, reaching to squeeze my hand.

There now, I thought—physical contact. We had shaken hands when we first met, but that was a social grace not open to interpretation. This was different. She deliberately touched me. It was an innocent gesture, correct for the moment, by no means suggestive or forward. But if the handshake is the first stage of a relationship, and if intimacy is third, then innocent touching must be second.

"That was easy enough," I said, referring to the invitation, "but I'm here for two reasons. I have a request."

"Oh?"

"Your seminar. I've read that your topic this fall will be 'Philosophy of Performance.' I wonder if I might audit your class. As an actor, I'd find your insights useful. I could put your ideas to work onstage. What do you think?"

At first she said nothing, leaving me to squirm. With a quizzical look, she finally answered, "I honestly don't know the school's policy on auditing—I'm new at this, remember. As far as I know, the course is filled. But I'll find out. If it's possible, you'll be admitted. I'd like that, George."

". . . thank you," I stammered, hardly believing my ears.

"Now, how about that drink you've politely refused?"

"Thank you, Claire, but I have to be going. Really."

"Then at least let me bring the wine next weekend. Red?"

"Perfect. Casual, you know—just the three of us, just friends. Can we expect you around eight?"

"With bells on. And I'll have a decision for you about the seminar by then."

Now it's Saturday, it's eight o'clock, classes start next week, and I haven't heard a word. I'm getting nervous.

"George," says Guy, "sorry to intrude on your ice-sucking, but there are a few things to do before she gets here. Let's see. The vinaigrette is done. I assume you want the salad after the meat course . . ."

The doorbell interrupts him. We stare at each other as if commanded to freeze.

"Christ." A lump forms in my throat as I leave the kitchen, retucking my shirt on the way, stopping at the hall mirror to rake my fingers through my hair. I wipe my palms on my hips and reach for the doorknob as the bell rings again.

"Claire!" I say with a broad smile as I swing the door open, leaning forward to exchange a kiss on the cheek, noting the easy progress of our innocent touching.

"Good evening, dear," she says as she steps over the threshold, offering me a little shopping bag that holds two bottles of wine—good stuff, French, with unfamiliar but impressive labels.

"Thank you, how nice. I didn't hear you drive up."

"I walked. It's good for me."

"But I thought Kiki left you her car."

"She did, but . . ." She stops, having thought of something, then asks, "Can you drive a car with a clutch?"

"Well, sure." I'm confused by the question, but remind myself of how women often wallow in their helplessness. "Sure, I drive stick."

"Perhaps, if you wouldn't mind—could you take it out now and then? Kiki seems to think it's important."

"I'd be happy to. But hell, why don't I teach you to drive it? Mastering a clutch is no big deal."

"It is if you've never driven; I don't have a license. We'll talk about it later," she says brightly, dismissing the topic. "Now show me what you've done here."

She strolls from the hall into the living room and is drawn at
once to my most treasured piece, a Louis XV-style ebony
escritoire. Too small to be used as a desk, its top displays some
of my better objets. Next to a three-candle bouillote lamp is an
antique Cartier writing set—leather blotter, crystal inkstand, and
ormolu letter opener—all sporting a monogram not my own.
Atop the blotter is a Georgian tea caddy, a little chest of fine
burled walnut with brass handles and lock. Claire lifts the box,
examines its workmanship, and replaces it on the desk, disturb-
ing my tablescape.

She crosses the room to admire a pair of Hepplewhite lolling
chairs, with seats and backs of silvery damask strié, flanking a
rolled-arm sofa. The steely glaze of its plump chintz cushions is
repeated in soft folds of curtains at both windows. Waning
daylight casts warm rectangles on the charcoal ground of a
needlepoint carpet. Claire clasps her hands, cooing her approval.

While she studies the room, I study her. Normally, a red linen
jumpsuit shouldn't be worn by a woman of Claire's age, but she
wears one this evening with taste and aplomb. Crisp at the collar,
bunched at the waist, properly wrinkled at the knees, it gives her
a vital look that belies her years. Anyone would call her a
"striking" woman, but it is obvious tonight that she was once very
pretty indeed.

"Very pretty indeed," she says of the room. "And your use of
grays is up-to-the-minute. Simply smashing. I don't think it looks
at all as if a couple of old ladies live here."

Guy has appeared from the dining room. Seizing the opportunity, I announce, "Speak of the devil—here's the other old lady
now."

"I resent that," Guy says with good-natured indignance.

"Claire, I'd like you to meet Guy Anderson. Guy, this is Claire
Gray."

"So happy to meet you, Miss Gray. Welcome to our home."

"Thank you, dear," she tells him as they join all four hands
and wiggle them, a curious mutation of a handshake. "We're all
friends here. Do call me Claire—and you're Guy."

"In case George hasn't mentioned it, Claire, your outfit's a
knockout."

"Oh?" she asks demurely, stepping back as if to check herself in a mirror. "Why, thank you, Guy."

I feel a tinge of annoyance that they've responded so well, so quickly, to each other, so I end their pleasantries by suggesting, "How about a drink? I'm concocting something special in the kitchen."

"How intriguing," says Claire. "What on earth is it?"

"It's called a Ramos fizz. It has nine ingredients if you count the ice."

"The Ramos gin fizz," she says wistfully. "A New Orleans drink, if I'm not mistaken. I first had one at Mardi Gras many years ago, and I've made them myself on rare occasions, though it's been ages. Mind if we watch?"

"Not at all," I tell her, pleased that she's enthused, but disappointed that she's familiar with the drink, which I only recently discovered.

As I lead them to the kitchen through the dining room, Claire marvels at the table, loves the crystal, can't believe I arranged the flowers. "You're really a jack-of-all-trades," she says to me.

"He even cuts his own hair," Guy tells her.

I slip into the kitchen with the wine, perturbed that this litany of my talents has not included acting.

Claire and Guy follow me, and we go to work on our batch of Ramos fizzes. I squeeze lemons and limes; Guy separates eggs; Claire measures cream, sugar, and gin. All these ingredients, a few drops of orange-flower water, and lots of ice go into the blender. With a fillip toward the machine, Claire commands, "Grind away, maestro."

I switch it on, and we grit our teeth while the ice is pulverized. After a few moments, the racket calms to a hum, and the now-creamy mixture swirls heavily in its container. I pour the froth into three big glasses, topping each off with a slug of club soda, which reemerges as a head of foam.

"This calls for a toast," says Guy, serving Claire.

"That's easy," I tell them. "To Claire, to her stay in Evanstown, and most important, to her new play."

We touch glasses, then savor the concoction. Claire lowers her glass and licks her lips, missing the thin white moustache that has appeared under her nose. "Perfect," she decrees. "The texture is divine."

Guy and I agree. With no further conversation, we empty our

glasses. I suggest, "Another batch?"

"Absolutely," says Claire.

"Okay," I tell them, "while I work on the drinks, Guy can fire up the grill. And Claire, could you open the wine to breathe? There are corkscrews in the top drawer."

Guy steps out the back door, I crack an egg over the blender, and Claire chooses a corkscrew—the kind that waiters use, which I have never mastered. She zips the tin from the neck of each bottle, drives the screw into the first cork with several sharp twists, then slides it out with a quiet pop. Unpretentiously, she sniffs the cork. Satisfied, she proceeds with the second bottle.

"You're awfully good at that," I tell her.

"Experience." She grins. "There now. My job's done; how about yours?"

"Ready to rip, but let's wait for Guy."

"Of course. He seems so nice. You must be very happy together."

"Happy enough." My answer is deliberately vague.

"Hm." Her brow wrinkles as she looks into my eyes.

"Fire's going," Guy announces as he steps in from the back door, clapping grime from his hands. "We can start the meat soon. Any progress on that fizz?"

I answer by switching on the blender. When the glasses are distributed and we've tasted our second drink, I suggest, "How about some music? Any requests, Claire?"

"Oh, nothing too challenging, I should think. Something that will segue nicely into dinner."

Guy asks her, "Would you care to look at the records and CDs? George's collection is mostly pop; I'm into classical. You're sure to find something you like."

She says she'd be delighted to choose, so Guy escorts her to the other room, where he tells her, "The top shelf is classical—alphabetical by composer. Popular stuff's on the bottom—solo performers first, then groups, then shows." He switches on the equipment and returns to the kitchen, leaving her to browse.

"Everything under control out here?" he asks me.

"I've cleared our cocktail debris, so now we can get down to business. Could you get the tenderloin from the fridge, pretty please, and dredge it in the cracked pepper? You know how I hate handling meat."

"No comment . . . ," he says in a lilting, bitchy whisper.

We cackle mischievously as I begin work on the béarnaise.

The opening chords of a piano piece burst from the silence of the other room. Claire has chosen something of Guy's—Rachmaninoff, I think.

"Something smells marvelous," she says as she reappears in the kitchen.

"Something *sounds* marvelous," Guy tells her.

"Ashkenazy!" she gushes, flailing her hands in imitation of the arpeggios from the other room. "The man's a genius."

"A wonderful choice," says Guy.

"Wonderful choice," I echo with tepid enthusiasm.

"I'm astounded by your collection," she tells us. "Everything's so beautifully catalogued, so easy to find."

"Guy can take credit for that," I admit. "He's chief librarian. But between you and me, Claire, he gets fanatic about keeping the records straight. I just like to play them."

This draws a predictable response from Guy: "You can't very well play records if you can't find them, can you?"

His testy tone brings Claire to the rescue. "Of course not," she tells him soothingly. "You've done a magnificent job, and I'm sure George appreciates it, at least in his heart of hearts." She prompts me with a wink.

"I do, Guy. Truly. That sort of rigid organization . . . well, my mind doesn't work that way. But I'm glad yours does."

He eyes me for a moment, then allows himself a little grin. A truce has been reached.

Happy to change the subject, Claire says to me, "If Guy is chief librarian, you must be chief cook."

"And bottle washer," I add with a long-suffering sigh.

"Don't believe it," Guy cautions Claire. "I've never seen him wash a bottle. He throws away his empties."

We indulge in a round of laughter. The music has shifted from its austere opening section to lighter, more melodic passages. Its playfulness is infectious. We chatter away, trading quips and sarcasms while preparing our meal. Claire has insisted that we allow her to help, so we've put her to work peeling potatoes.

"I must warn you," she says, "that I'm far handier with a corkscrew than I am with a potato peeler." Lending credence to her words, the potato she's holding pops out of her hands and lands in the sink with a splat.

At long last, our production moves to the dining room. The meat has been grilled and sauced. The record is flipped, wine poured. Guy and I seat Claire, then ourselves.

"Now it's my turn," Claire says while raising her glass. "Such a beautiful meal, beautiful evening. So a toast: To my new friends."

We taste the wine. Claire has closed her eyes to more thoroughly appreciate it. Guy simply nods his approval. I feel I should comment, but being unfamiliar with the argot of winetasting—in which Claire is surely fluent—I choose my words with care. "I hope the rest of the meal measures up to the wine," I tell her.

"I'm sure it will put my simple wine to shame."

With the niceties out of the way, we devour dinner. Mr. Ashkenazy's piano is interrupted only by the clatter of cutlery and random sighs of satisfaction.

At this point—when everyone is seated, eating, and content—I'm usually able to relax. But not tonight. The purpose of this soirée is to make sure I get into Claire's seminar. It's getting late, and the subject hasn't been broached.

I clear my throat. "I imagine you're getting excited, Claire. Classes start next week."

"Excited, no. Scared, yes."

"Scared?" Guy asks her. "Nothing to fear—they're only college students."

"Easy for you to say, but I haven't set foot in a classroom for thirty years. What do you teach?" she asks him, veering from my intended topic. "English, isn't it?"

"That's right. You and I will both report to Connie."

"We're in the same line of work, then."

"Hardly!" I interrupt her with a laugh. "Your grad seminar is a far cry from Guy's classes. He teaches freshmen."

"Honors freshmen," he corrects me.

Claire turns to ask me, "Exactly what is it *you* do, George?" She forks the last bit of meat from her plate and drags it through the sauce. "I know you're a designer, but what does that entail, day to day?"

"Yes, George," Guy adds with a taunting smile, "tell us about Potter's."

"I'd rather not talk about . . . the office," I tell them blandly. "It's such a drudge, just a job. But my *life*—like yours, Claire—my life is the theater."

She smiles oddly, but says nothing.

The record has finished playing, and the needle skips in its last groove, punctuating the passing seconds with a slow, rhythmic thud.

"Uh, George," Guy says, breaking the lull, "why don't you tell Claire about your next play?"

"Excellent idea," I tell him, surprised he suggested it. While Guy rises from his chair to change the record, I explain to Claire, "Our local theater group, the Evanstown Players, has cast its fall production. I got the male lead."

"Congratulations. What's the play?"

"Just a comedy. Crowd-pleasing fluff. Noel Coward."

"Fluff, maybe, but divinely sophisticated fluff. You'll have a ball."

"Would you consider coming to see it, Claire? It would be a thrill for the whole cast, especially for me."

"I wouldn't think of missing it. I'll be directing a play next spring, and I need to scout the local talent for my own cast." As she finishes speaking, she winks at me.

She has plans for me. I can tell.

Guy has selected a new record—guitar music, light and pretty, perfect background for our conversation. Returning from the other room, he says to Claire, "I heard you mention your play. How's it going?"

"I haven't started writing yet, but the ideas have begun to crystallize. I'm still worried about the tone or 'voice' of the play. I want to make a point—I want to *say* something—but I don't want to sermonize."

Guy asks, "Can you tell us about it?"

She thinks a moment. "I'd rather not. The play will speak for itself, if I ever get it written. Suffice it to say, writers generally write about the things they know best, the people and places around them. But I'm learning it's better not to discuss my ideas. I learned that lesson a month ago at Dody and Camille's reception—those people stunted my thinking by weeks."

"I knew it!" I tell her with a hearty laugh.

Guy explains, "George thinks that educators are a bunch of

stuffed shirts."

"Present company excluded, pumpkin, they *are*."

"Perhaps," Claire agrees, remembering the party. "Stodgy people are more boring than bothersome, but some of those people simply weren't civil. Your psychiatrist's friend—Nigel Slough?—such a confused and irrational young man."

"I'd prefer to call Nigel a bit of a prick, if you'll pardon my French. He stops at nothing to satisfy his own inflated ego. He's the only man I know with a truly vicious sense of humor, the type who cracks jokes about AIDS."

Guy tells Claire, "We don't find much humor in that topic."

Looking him in the eye, she reaches over the table to rest her fingers on his arm. She says quietly, "Neither do we."

Guy returns her glance, then drops his eyes. "I'm sorry," he tells her. "Of course you don't."

Claire leans back in her chair and folds her hands in her lap. While Guy recovers from his gaffe, I fight the tension that grips my throat. Anxiety rises sharply as I ponder Claire's seminar. With an uncertain voice, I ask, "Anyone ready for salad?"

"That would be nice," says Claire. "May I help?"

Guy and I refuse her offer and stand to clear the table. While rising from my chair, I tug the wrinkles from the lap of my jeans. And I notice Claire—watching my hands.

We take the dishes to the kitchen. Guy begins rinsing them while I arrange the salad plates. He tells me, "Forgot the butter dish."

I return to the dining room, where Claire relaxes with a cigarette between courses. The butter is at the far end of the table. Instead of walking around for it, I plant myself at Claire's side and lean to reach, practically brushing my hips in her face. Her eyes widen and smoke darts from her nostrils as she coughs petitely. Retrieving the butter, I flash her an innocent smile and retreat to the kitchen.

"Keeping Claire amused?" Guy asks.

"She seems content," I tell him smugly, pleased with myself, pleased with my game. But my emotions are mixed. I feel panicky, wondering about her class, pondering the fate of my plan. I am slipping into a depression when I hear her enter the room. I turn at the sound of her voice.

"George," she says from the doorway, raising a hand to stifle a laugh. "I'd almost forgotten—how silly of me! You need to know about the seminar."

"Oh, *that*. I'd forgotten, too," I tell her, mimicking her laugh. "What's up?"

"It's no problem. The class meets at my place, and I don't need permission to have you in my own home."

"Claire, that's wonderful. When do we meet?"

"Monday evenings, seven till nine."

"My God, that's the day after tomorrow. Is there anything I need to read first? I don't think I'm ready."

"You're ready," she says coyly. "But how about that salad?"

"*Oui, madame. Zee salahd is finis,*" I tell her in a ridiculous accent. Then, dropping it, "And wait till you taste it—Guy does a fabulous vinaigrette."

M onday morning, a nervous wreck. Woke up with a knot in my throat. Dreamed about Claire's seminar, the first meeting tonight. Dreading it, but certain I'll be there, older than the others.

Running late. Too long in the shower. Doc Solomon may be a simple country shrink, but he charges two bucks a minute, and I'm waltzing into his office five minutes late. His receptionist glances up from her bookkeeping, jots something in her ledger, and jerks her head toward the inner office.

As I enter, Solomon rises from behind his desk, where he's been studying a file, presumably mine. He extends his hand, says, "Good morning, George," does not check his watch, does not mention that I'm late. "Chair or couch today?"

"Better lie down. Lots to sort out."

He nods. Taking a notebook from his desk, he sits in the chair I normally use.

I don't like the couch. I try folding my arms, then crossing my ankles. I feel exposed. I'd like a blanket.

"Whenever you care to begin . . . ," he prompts me.

"It's back. The choking."

"*Globus hystericus.* You sense a lump in your throat. A classic anxiety symptom, a form of mild hysteria."

"Not so mild," I correct him. "I'm a wreck this morning."

"Did this come out of the blue, or can you identify what

triggered it?"

"I have a meeting tonight, and it's got me jumpy. I have to go, want to go, but I'm scared. I need to calm down."

Having stated the problem, I pause, pressing my fingertips to my forehead. I wait for the doctor's reassuring words, wait to hear that the choking will disappear when the cause of the anxiety has passed.

But he is silent for an uncomfortably long time, until at last he says, "You're doing it again, George. You're after a quick fix."

"I'm not asking for drugs."

"I didn't say you were. But you've come here with another of your daily crises, and you expect me to patch things up. I'm not a short-term therapist; I'm an analyst. We made that distinction when we began these sessions."

"Well, *excuse me.*" Roused by his scolding tone, I sit up and face him squarely from the couch. "I'm sorry if my 'daily crises' bore you, but let's remember who's the customer here, and let's remember what they say about customers. Maybe it's time for me to shop elsewhere."

"Maybe it is," he agrees calmly. "Look, George, you and I have a problem: This analysis isn't working. We've been at it two years, we're going in circles, and there's no end in sight. During effective analysis, the patient must cross a series of hurdles. Each is simply an insight, a discovery based on self-examination. You haven't crossed your first hurdle because you're not willing to look at yourself. Perhaps we should quit trying. These sessions have become a frustration for me and a financial burden for you."

Seething, I snap at him, "Listen, doctor, you're paid to endure the frustration. And if you don't mind, let *me* worry about the expense. I pay my bills."

"Guy pays them. He writes me a check every month."

I laugh. "That doesn't mean anything. We have a joint account, and Guy takes care of the finances."

"I don't know who you think you're kidding, or why, and I certainly don't care how I get paid. But I do care that you seem to believe the stories you concoct, that you can't draw the line between reality and fantasy, between truth and lies."

"You're preaching," I tell him. "Knock it off. Professionals don't pass judgment, remember? Besides, who the hell are you to preach? Would anyone of truly sound mind choose to live with

Nigel Slough? Heal thyself, buster."

"I don't live with Nigel." His voice is strained, patience stretched. "I sleep with him."

"Everyone does that," I tell him with wide, innocent eyes. I can't resist adding, "Think I haven't?"

He glares at me, unable to decide which epithet to spit first. His temples throb visibly. But he says nothing. Instead, he closes his eyes.

When at last he opens them, he tells me, "I'm not perfect; no one is. Nigel certainly isn't. In spite of his arrogance and his sometimes cruel behavior, I find him highly attractive. I like him for all the wrong reasons—the superficial nonsense of youth and beauty—but I offer no apologies. Yes, Nigel is a problem, but he's my problem."

He pauses a moment, then continues, "There now. We've agreed that I have shortcomings. But you've come here, George, to discuss your own problems. And this is crucial: My weaknesses do not disqualify me from analyzing yours. I have no desire to judge or preach. When I say you're unwilling to take an honest look at yourself, when I warn of the danger in believing your own lies, that's not a sermon, but a diagnosis."

I'm watching him quietly. He has spoken firmly but not in anger. Calmer now, I fold my hands in my lap, scratching my thumbs together. "I'm not sure what you mean," I tell him. "Honesty, lies? I'm willing to look at myself. It took me a while to *find* myself, sure—but having done that, I've never denied my real nature. I'm no closet queen."

Having laid the issue bare, I expect him to praise me for crossing my first hurdle, but he tells me flatly, "Homosexuality isn't the root of your problem. Granted, gay life in a straight world is rife with game playing and self-denial. We straddle the line, choosing either truth to what we are or obeisance to what others expect of us. But everyone faces that dilemma. Man, the social animal, compromises himself again and again, trading bits of his true nature for acceptance by the larger group. Homosexuals may feel forced to play this game more vigorously than heterosexuals, and this can exact a considerable emotional toll. But the fact is, George, you play this survival game quite well."

"Maybe I should feel relieved," I tell him with a humorless laugh, "but I'm more confused than ever."

"Lie down again, George, and close your eyes. Forget our quarrel. We won't cross any hurdles today, but we made a decent try, for once. We've got some time left, so tell me about this meeting you're dreading."

"It's a class. Claire Gray's seminar begins tonight."

"But you're not in the graduate program; you're not even a student. How'd you get in?"

I prop myself on one elbow to look at him. "Claire asked me to audit. We're close personal friends."

"Now, George. I know for a fact that you first met her at Doddson Henry's only a few weeks ago."

"Just this weekend, she came over to the house for dinner, and she asked me to sit in on her course."

"I should think you'd be delighted."

"I am." Letting my head fall back on the cushion, I stare at the ceiling as I tell him, "But I'm afraid I'll seem out of place. I'm so much older than the kids who'll be there."

"Those 'kids' are grad students, into their twenties."

"And I'm nearly forty, old enough to be their father."

"You? A father, George? Don't be silly."

Affecting a lisp, I ask him, "Silly? What's so silly about that?"

"You claim to have sired a child, and it may be true, but no one in Evanstown is convinced of it."

"You want pictures?"

"Of course not. Point is, you were more of a father to that dog buried under the birdbath than you were to any child, real or imagined."

Trying to control my defensive tone, I explain, "Butch was a pedigreed weimaraner, a prince among dogs, man's best friend. The child . . . , well, I never really got to know her. She was very young. And her mother was one holy terror. Yes, doctor," I sum it up with a rude laugh, "Butch was a prince, but mummy was the bitch."

"I see," he says tersely, no humor in his voice. "It was her fault. Your ex-wife."

"It sure as hell was." I'm getting angry. Didn't want to talk about this. Have other problems.

Solomon takes a minute to scribble on his pad. When a calmer mood has settled over us, he asks, "If the seminar has you so worried, why go?"

"It's not a question of going or not. I *have* to go." When he gazes back at me with a confused expression, I decide to be open with him. "It's part of the plan."

"What plan?"

"Claire Gray is here in Evanstown to write a play. I plan to star in it. So I wangled myself into her seminar. It's the perfect way to get close to her and clinch the role."

"Hold on. I thought she *asked* you to take the class."

"Oh. Right, she did. And it was great, the way it fit the plan."

"I don't get it, George. Why the scheme? She's got all year to discover that you're the best actor in town. Just be yourself, do your best, and try out for the part. If you're right for the role, you'll undoubtedly get it."

"No, doc, I've got to make sure. You're not thinking big enough. It's time to think beyond Evanstown. The point of the plan is to get out of here. If I succeed, Claire will take me to New York and cast me on Broadway."

Solomon is watching me with a cynical gaze that erupts into laughter as he asks, "How you gonna pull *that* off? Plan to sleep with her?"

"If I have to."

He laughs all the harder, thumping one foot. He finds this phase of my plan so hilarious, I expect him to start slapping his knee. But when he glances at my face and sees that I'm taking no part in his merriment, his laughter stops short. Catching his breath, he stares into my eyes and says in a monotone, "You're not joking."

"Of course not."

He holds his stare for a moment, then looks away. Through puckered lips he blows a long, breathy sigh, almost a whistle. He poises his pen over his notebook, but words escape him. He flips the pen between his fingers and begins tapping its other end on the paper. He squirms in his chair.

"George, let's think about this. Don't you see that your plan is fraught with emotional pitfalls? Think of Claire and how you'd be using her. Think of Guy and how you'd be hurting him. And if these mawkish considerations mean nothing to you, take a cold, critical look at the logic of your scheme. Quite frankly, it's flawed. I remember reading somewhere that if Claire Gray takes her play to Broadway, Arnold . . . "

"*Look*, doctor," I interrupt him. "Here I am, suffering and anxiety-ridden, in the throes of acute mid-life crisis. I've come to you for help, for relief, and what do I get? Guilt trips. You're preaching again, and I don't like it."

"Preaching?" he asks in a shrill voice. "You're damn right I'm preaching."

I've seen him excited before, and I've seen him upset, but I've never seen Doctor Solomon angry. Now he's angry.

"Why shouldn't I preach when you won't look at reality, won't listen to reason? Do you understand that you wield the capacity to hurt people, including yourself? It's cruel to hurt others, and it's stupid to hurt yourself. If you expect me to coddle you and encourage your scheming—I won't, because that wouldn't help you. I had hoped, through our sessions, to point you in a direction that might relieve your anxiety attacks. But anxiety is merely a symptom. To eliminate the symptom, we have to get to its root and deal honestly, ruthlessly with the deeper problem. I can't deal with that problem because you're not being honest with me. Far worse, you're not being honest with yourself."

He falls silent. I ponder his words. Disgusted, I finally tell him, "I don't know what the hell you're talking about."

"Honestly? You honestly don't understand? Then let me state it plainly: This analysis has failed, and these sessions are through. Give me a call sometime—when you're ready to look at the world as it really is."

The students, about a dozen, gather their things and prepare to leave. It's Monday night, nine o'clock. Claire's seminar has ended. While handing out a list of readings for our second meeting, she says to me in a detached, professional tone, "Mr. McBeth, could you stay late a few minutes? I have something for you."

Seated on the edge of the stage in Claire's living room, watching the others leave, I wonder what she might have. As the last student closes the door, leaving Claire and me alone, the phone rings.

With an apologetic shrug, she retreats to the far end of the room and answers the phone crisply, "Yes?" Her impatience is transformed to delight as she recognizes her caller. "Manny! Hello, darling. Yes, it just ended. Not badly at all, thank you."

While she gabs with her caller, I'm left with my thoughts. The seminar, which had filled me with such dread, was painless and interesting. The two hours passed quickly, with the group quizzing Claire on her experiences in the theater. Future meetings will be more structured, now that she's assigned readings. Glancing over the list in my hand, I cringe at the dull, academic titles. I'm sure I won't read them.

"Yes, Manny, I'm ready to begin writing," she says into the phone. "The thematic ideas have been cooking long enough, and now I've hit upon a plot. Since last weekend, it's really started to click. I'll begin my outline tomorrow."

As they continue talking, the topic shifts from her play to a movie. Just who *is* this character on the phone? At last she tells him, "I hate to seem rude, dear, but I must be going." She pauses, then laughs. "As a matter of fact, I'm not alone." She winks at me. "A student? Of course not." She laughs again, promises to stay in touch, and hangs up.

"Manny's such a dear," she tells me, gliding across the room. "He knew how nervous I was about the class, so he phoned to make sure I'd survived. He's been so supportive—but then, he *should* be," she tells me in a tone of grave understatement, as if her meaning couldn't be more obvious. "Well," she asks, changing subjects, "what did you think of the class?"

"I had no idea what to expect, and I was probably more nervous than you were. But my fears were groundless. The class was a joy, you were magnificent, and your *reading* assignments—can't wait to sink my teeth into those essays."

She eyes me askance. "Let's not go overboard, George. Most of it's pretty dry, but it's valuable background, so I hope you'll spend some time with it."

"If you say it's important, I'll plod through."

"Wonderful. Now, how about a drink? We've managed to cope with this nerve-racking experience, and I think we deserve to celebrate." She leads me toward the back of the room, where a sleek row of cabinets houses a well-stocked bar. "I have something to give you," she reminds me, "and we're apt to find it here." She plucks a tiny blue bottle from among the many others. Presenting its label as though it were a fine wine, she says, "For you, my dear. Orange-flower water."

"You shouldn't have," I tell her, delighted by her thoughtfulness.

"Just a thank-you for entertaining me so regally last weekend. You were running low, and it's sometimes hard to find." Wrinkling her brow, she asks, "Is it autumn yet?"

Puzzled by the nonsequitor, I tell her, "I'm not sure. Next week, I guess."

"Good. Cooler weather signals the start of the Scotch-drinking season. I've been vacillating for weeks, and it's time to take a stand." She fills two glasses with a few ice cubes, then pours the Scotch—the good stuff, the unblended kind. She hands me a glass, clicks hers to mine, then drinks.

I do likewise, shuddering as the whiskey assaults my tongue. She, by contrast, breathes a happy sigh, as though she'd swallowed nectar smooth as silk.

"Let's get comfortable and talk," she suggests. "It's impossible down here, unless you have a perverse affinity for carpeted cubes, so let's go upstairs."

Drinks in hand, we climb to the first balcony, arriving in a modern kitchen with a Parsons dining table. In a corner of the loft is a grouping of upholstered furniture. This must be where Claire spends much of her time, judging from the clutter of magazines and newspapers, the ashtray and cigarettes, the pair of shoes at the base of an overstuffed chair.

Suggesting that we sit, she arranges herself in the big chair, slipping off her shoes and dropping them near the others. Leaning to one side, she pulls her feet onto the seat and tucks her toes into the cushion.

I sit at the end of the sofa, near her chair. Feet on the floor, knees spread, I hold my drink between my legs.

She watches silently for a moment, then smiles and tells me, "I'm glad you're here."

"So am I." I return her smile and sip the Scotch. "Do you miss New York?"

"Not really. I needed to get away, but I'll return in due time. It's not as though I'm in exile."

"Evanstown may be a nice place to visit, but living here *is* like exile."

"Aren't we being a tad dramatic?" She raises her brows in an expression of frankness. "New York's just down the track. Train leaves every day. If you feel thwarted here, you should get away now and then."

"I do. I go to New York at least once a year."

"Oh? Theater?"

"Mainly." I reach to touch my glass to hers, saying, "I've seen all your latest shows. Most recently, *Inner Moments*. It was terrific. And Arnold Manley—he's something else. But they've *all* been great, I'm sure."

"You'd be surprised," she tells me with a low laugh. "Let's see now. You go to plays in New York. What else do you do in the city?"

"Museums, usually."

She eyes me in a way that says she wasn't born yesterday.

"And bars, of course. I do the bars." Unsure of how she might react, I add, "And sometimes, the parks."

"Have you been to the Ramble?"

"Claire! You're not supposed to know about that."

"C'mon," she says, suddenly street-wise, "I'm not stupid, you know. I live in the neighborhood. I have friends." She leans forward and says in a quieter, confidential tone, "So 'fess up. What goes on in there?"

Laughing, I tell her, "I admit nothing. Those antics are either illegal, contagious, or both."

"Thank God for penicillin, eh?"

I shrug. "I'm skeptical of God and allergic to penicillin, which isn't the cure-all it used to be. So I place my faith in our local VD clinic. They patch up the sinner without condemning the sin, and they hand out condoms like candy. I go in for a blood test every month or so."

She eyes me ever-so-innocently. "Been checked lately?"

I return her gaze for a moment before telling her, "I'm clean." I'm nervous, too. Our conversation has taken a turn that points the evening toward an unexpected climax. I'm not sure I'm ready, but it's part of the plan. Been saving it. Look confident. Smile.

"You shouldn't chew ice," she tells me. "Your smile's far too beautiful to risk cracking a tooth." She rises from her chair and takes my glass. "I think you need a refill."

As she descends to the lower level, I rise from the sofa to ask, "Can I be of any help?"

She looks up from a turn of the spiral stairs. "As a matter of fact, you can. Not down here, though." She points to the higher balcony. "Can you guess what's up there?"

"I have an inkling."

"No, not that. Upstairs is Kiki's costume collection. There's a problem with the lighting. Focus and color—it's all wrong. It needs your eye. Could you check it out?"

While Claire goes to the bar, I climb to the upper loft. "My God," I mutter as I catch my first glimpse.

There's a bed, of course—a stepped platform, kind of a stage, a real playpen. But the dominant feature of the room is the collection. Eight or ten racks extend from the back wall with aisles between. Hundreds of costumes dangle to the floor. Many are part of Kiki's goofy street wardrobe, but most are period theater costumes. Above the racks are shelves heaped with hats, wigs, masks, the works.

Equally unexpected is the view. From the edge of the loft, I peer over the main room and through the huge window, thirty feet high, at the lights of Evanstown. They sparkle through the trees, through the spires and towers of the campus, ending abruptly at the bottom of the valley, where the placid surface of Evans Run shimmers beneath a September moon.

Stepping back, I notice the fireplace. Its chimney rises to the ceiling, where suspended tracks hold an array of theatrical lighting. Claire was right; the effect is wrong. The fixtures are focused on the costume collection, which destroys the mood of the loft as a bedroom. Some of the lights are unfiltered, which is too harsh, while others are gelled in various shades of blue, which is too cold.

Music begins playing throughout the house. Sprightly and classical, it's probably Mozart.

"What do you think?" Claire asks, coming up the stairs with our drinks, which are filled higher than before.

"The view is stunning," I tell her, "but you're right—the lights need work."

"Good," she says, handing me my glass. "Let's fix them."

She explains the circuits that control the loft, flipping switches, twirling dimmers. "And I imagine you'll need these," she says, producing a box of gels. She rolls a stepladder from between two racks of costumes and positions it beneath a row of lights. With a wave of her hand, she offers, "Be my guest."

She relaxes with her drink at the foot of the bed. Eyeing me as I climb the ladder, she comments, "Nice view." I stumble on the next step.

I've often aimed and filtered lights for the stage, but never in a home. I'm amazed how quickly the room is transformed. Dragging the ladder around the loft, up and down, new focus, new gels, a sensitive hand on the dimmers—and presto. The emphasis is no longer on the costumes, but on the bed. It seems to float on a pool of pink haze. When I descend the ladder for the last time and roll it away to a now-darkened corner, Claire says, "This is exactly what I had in mind."

"A definite improvement," I agree. Having worked up a sweat under the lights, I unbutton my shirt and pull its tail from my pants. "Now we're going to play a little game."

"Oh?" she asks from the edge of the bed.

"We're going to play Name That Gel. You have to tell me—precisely—what color I've used."

"You're playing with a pro, kiddo," she warns me. Looking into the lights, she decrees, "It's not one of the reds, and it's no shade of pink. That's 'bastard amber.'"

"Damn. You *are* good."

"An adroit guess," she confesses. "Now why don't you get comfortable? Sit here by me." She pats the bed.

"Can I light the fire first? It'll complete the mood."

"A fire? I thought you were warm, having virtually stripped to the waist."

"I merely unbuttoned my shirt." Turning my back to her, I slip the shirt off one shoulder in a silly, coquettish manner, then let it drop to the floor. "Better?"

"Light your damn fire," she tells me, trying to sound bored by the display of my torso. "It's one of those gas-log affairs. Turn it on slowly—it sort of explodes."

As instructed, I hold a match between the logs until the gas ignites with a frightening thud.

"That's nice," she says, unalarmed. Then her tone turns comically impatient. She punctuates each word by pounding the mattress: "Now—please—sit—down."

"Yes, ma'am." I slip off my shoes at the edge of the bed and sit next to her, primly at first. After reaching to the floor to pick up my drink, I lie on my side, propped by an elbow, looking into the fire.

Long moments pass. The setting is romantic, potentially erotic. Pink lights above, sparkling lights of the town beyond, moonlight slicing across the wall. Civilized music as if from nowhere, the tranquil relic of another age.

She is at my side, very near, but I'm aware only of myself. I study my body, entranced by the fire, its glow on my chest. My jeans are tight. Getting tighter.

"When you go to New York . . . ," she says, reminding me I'm not alone. A note of reticence colors her voice. "Does Guy go with you?"

"Of course not," I tell her, laughing at the question. "I book my trips while Guy's tied up with school."

"The bars and parks—does he know about them?"

"He's a clever lad."

"Doesn't that hurt him terribly?" she asks, jabbing a fingernail between her teeth.

"It doesn't," I assure her.

She forgoes her finger and drains the last of her Scotch.

"He and I have an open relationship—as open as we dare these days. Fidelity was never part of the bargain. Tonight as I was leaving for class, Guy told me, 'Have fun. I won't wait up.' Can you imagine?"

With the finger she'd been biting, she swirls the ice in her empty glass. Then she looks me in the eye and accuses me baldly, "You lie."

I finish my drink and put the glass on the floor. Flopping back onto the bed, I stretch my arms languidly over my head and dig my shoulder blades into the satin of the comforter. I'm getting excited, feeling turned-on. I can well imagine the effect my posing must have on Claire.

She asks, "Can I get you another drink?"

"Sure." But liquor is the least of my desires. My mind is locked between my legs. She's gone. She's risen from the bed and taken our glasses downstairs. I'm alone. My fingers unbutton my jeans, zip open the fly. Standing now, dizzy, not used to unblended Scotch. I slip out of my clothes and grip myself. Feel it grow in my hand.

Where is she? Can't hear her. The music has stopped. She's switched off the lights downstairs. Fully aroused, I want to come, get it over, go home. But no, it's part of the plan. Better save it.

Better put something on. She'd be horrified to find me naked, waiting in her bedroom. I'll search the costume collection for a caftan, a kimono, something loose.

Fingering thróugh the first row of hangers, I quickly lose interest in finding a simple smock. My eye is drawn to a bolero. The tiny jacket of pink silk has a collar and lapels of stiff black lace, epaulets dangling with beaded fringe. I yank it from its hanger and try it on. Covering only my back and shoulders, its rakish cut reveals most of my chest, its ruffled sleeves stop just above my elbows. Rifling the upper shelf, I find a long pair of black embroidered gloves. While slipping them on, I spot the mask. I lift it reverently and look into the holes of its wide, sequined eyes—catlike, feminine, sinister. Wearing only the bolero and gloves, I decide the mask will complete my costume. I strap it to my face and peer through its eyes, now my own.

"Seems we had the same idea," Claire says from behind.

Looking over my shoulder, I see her at the top of the stairs, holding the cocktails. She is naked. Lean and handsome, she shows herself openly.

I tell her, "Lost your clothes, lady," in case this detail has escaped her attention.

Laughing hard, she throws back her head to swallow lungfuls of air. But as I turn and approach her for my drink, her laughter stops short. A jolt of disbelief knocks the glasses from her hands. They shatter on the metal stairs and fall in shards, ice and whiskey littering the lower levels of the house. She stares at me, motionless.

"What's wrong?" I ask. "The mask?"

"No," she stammers, raising both palms as if warding off something evil, "no, not the mask." Dropping the last vestige of her finishing-school decorum, she tells me, "It's . . . your cock."

My turn to laugh. With hands on hips to more fully display the object of her amazement, I exhale loud chortles, shaking the fringe of my epaulets.

"Very funny," she pouts.

"Look," I tell her as my laughter wanes, "I don't intend to *rape* you. The decision's yours. You wouldn't be the first to back down after having a peek."

She watches while I stroke myself. With crossed arms and a snort of defiance, she says, "I'll take that challenge."

"Very good, madam," I tell her with a deferential bow. Waving toward the costumes, I ask, "Before we begin, may I entice you with something from the Kiki Collection? Lingerie, perhaps? Or are studs and buckles more to madam's liking?"

"No, thank you. I prefer sex like Scotch—straight, if you'll pardon the expression. You're welcome to adorn your body in any manner you wish, but it seems you've overlooked a crucial accessory."

From nowhere, she produces a condom, unwrapped and ready to roll. I comply.

Raising my arm in a courtly pose, I lead her toward the bed with slow, arching steps, as though preparing for a minuet. Grasping her hand, I lower her to lie before me on the comforter. Sprawled on the satin, her body looks weak and vulnerable, but fixed on her face is the wistful smirk of a conqueror.

There will be no foreplay. I climb onto the bed on all fours, straddle her legs with my knees, and crawl forward to look into her eyes. Trapped in the cage of my limbs, she peers back at me but cannot see the uncertainty in my eyes, masked by my costume and my posturing. With a tilt of my pelvis, I nudge my rubberized cock between her legs, which she parts reflexively. Holding my breath, I enter her.

A grimace, a wave of apprehension crosses her face when I slip past the lips of her vagina. Her body tenses beneath me as I press onward. When at last I'm lodged fully within, poised motionless above her, the tension leaves her body and a smile turns her mouth.

I lean close. "There's more than one way to ace *your* class, professor."

"You're only auditing, remember?"

"Wrong, professor. I'm auditioning."

"Hm. At least you're honest. At least sometimes."

During her last remark I have withdrawn, but now I slide back in, quickly. I hear her nails scratch the satin. Her head flops to one side as she inhales through clenched teeth. My second thrust produces no such reaction, and on the third, her breathing calms. By the fourth, she faces me with a blank stare of satisfaction. Finding the rhythm, finding my pace, slow and steady. Basic fuck.

I'd prefer to be tangled with Guy right now or, better yet, with one of the stud-students from tonight's seminar—the preppy number with the tight khaki ass would do nicely. But neither Guy nor the stud-student is handing out Broadway leads, so we'll stick to business.

Getting warm. The bolero is stuck to my skin. Sticking to business, picking up speed. Waiting for the switch, the flash that says you can't turn back.

She moans. Her pupils roll and she no longer sees me. I don't see her. I see myself. I watch through the eyes of a closeted spectator, indulging in the sight of long muscles that expand and contract within my thighs. It is I, not she, split open, victimized on an altar of satin. The winged shadow of my mask flutters like a bat in the pool of bastard amber spilling from the mattress to the floor.

Switch. Sex flash. Linkage of brain and groin. Arched back of a damned animal. Thinking of Guy. Won't be long. Thinking of stud-student. Tight khaki ass.

"Oh Guy," oh God, getting close.

"Christ," whine of pleasure, shriek of pain. Hers or mine?

Won't be long, getting close. Sweating hard, pounding hard. Pounding thinking. Khaki thinking. Pounding khaki ass.

Gripped by the rush of orgasm, my whole body stiffens, my rhythm breaks, I lunge, let it come. Collapse at her side.

Mingled sighs rise like smoke through pink fingers of light.

"Next time," she warns me while removing my mask and tossing it to the floor, "I won't be so passive. It's not my style."

"Any complaints?"

"A minor one. You never kissed me."

I lean over and kiss her on the lips.

"Rather perfunctory, George. But I shouldn't complain. If kissing's not your forte, I know what is."

Her tone has turned playful. While helping me remove the long gloves, she picks a wrestling match. Though spunky and quick, she knows her strength won't equal mine, so she resorts to tickling. Laughing and winded, we collapse side by side.

When she's caught her breath, she says to me, "I know where you live, what you do, what you've got between your legs. Otherwise, you're a mystery. Tell me about yourself."

"Okay," I tell her while sitting up to peel the sweaty bolero from my back. I nestle next to her again, extending an arm for her to use as a pillow. "All About Me. Funny, I was on a psychiatrist's couch just this morning. Didn't think I'd be analyzed again tonight."

"Stick to the subject."

"I was born nearly forty years ago in the Midwest—a small city, much smaller than New York but much bigger than Evanstown. It was an unremarkable place, but good for growing up, at a time when Dutch elms still arched every street. My father ran a small business, my mother took me to church, and I went to school. I was a good student, not a whiz, but a hard worker and well behaved, so I was always teacher's pet. Among my classmates, I enjoyed the reputation of a sissy.

"This distance from my 'peers'—and I use the word loosely—worried my parents. Since I showed no interest in little-boy pastimes, they began to fear that their one-and-only might not be inclined to pass on the family name. When I was in second or third grade, they tried to involve me in activities that would make a little man out of me.

"Bright one Saturday morning, my father announced it was time to think about Little League. *Huh?* I reminded him that baseball is played outdoors and that it requires sliding in the dirt. This was unacceptable. Besides, I didn't know beans about the game. What team would want me? No problem, he assured me—with all his business connections, I'd be in uniform in no time. *Uniform?* No way. I was adamant. Still, he appeared the next Saturday with a spanking new ball, bat, and mitt, begging me to give it a try. Out in the back yard, I laid it on thick, shrieking and cowering each time he threw the ball. After three or four pitches, he abandoned the idea.

"Mother didn't give up so easily. One day when I came home from school, she announced it was time to think about cub scouts. *Huh?* She'd gotten a letter from school telling her that dens were being organized. She wanted to sign me up and set me on the path to manliness. I argued that I had better things to do than burn marshmallows and whittle. She pleaded. I bluffed, saying I would become a cub scout if she would become a den mother. She was never a joiner or a club-type, so I knew this suggestion would settle the issue. But she called my bluff by taking a den and forcing me to join.

"We met on Tuesdays after school in our basement. All of us, including den mother, were expected to wear uniforms. I refused to wear the pants, ever, but conceded on the shirt for a few weeks because I liked the yellow scarf. It had a metal clasp that looked like a knot of golden rope. I thought of it as jewelry, and I loved it. But the clasp was scouting's sole reward. The rest was nonsense. We spent our afternoons stuck in the cellar trying to build birdhouses—I swear to God—out of Popsicle sticks and shellac.

"After a month, I'd had enough. Another boy from the den— a kindred spirit, I'm sure—would pledge allegiance, then slip upstairs with me to sip 'Coke-tails' from big wine glasses while browsing through my mother's decorating magazines. We'd let out horrified screams when a room didn't measure up to our standards, or coos of rapture when it did. So my mother was stuck in the dungeon folding flags for the rest of the year while I nurtured my budding interest in interiors.

"I spent Saturdays at the public library reading everything I could find on the topic, studying pictures of rooms, past and present. I discovered my own set of heroes, far different from the cowboys and jocks who were my classmates' idols. There was Elsie de Wolfe, a flamboyant turn-of-the-century decorator who founded the profession as we know it today. And Sister Parrish, the reigning queen of interiors for so many years. And Billy Baldwin, who established decorating as a *man's* job. I dreamed that someday I would join their ranks. At a holiday dinner, when relatives asked what I wanted to be when I grew up, my parents cringed as I announced: an interior decorator. I couldn't imagine anything more glamorous.

"Until high school. I discovered theater, loved it, and soon became the star of my school's drama club. Even though I was no good at sports, acting made me 'somebody,' and my path seemed clear. I would become an actor.

"But my parents wouldn't hear of it. 'Too iffy, too competitive,' they warned. Mom and pop now found themselves pushing me into decorating—even *that* seemed more palatable to their Midwestern mores than having a son who 'playacts.' So I enrolled in a respectable design program at a good Eastern school far, far from home.

"College, while it lasted, was a blast. Aside from classes, my principal activities were theater and sex. Theater was an old favorite, but sex was something new. I must have been a late bloomer. Any stirrings I felt in high school, I buried. But college was a fresh setting with new opportunities. From that first loving moment—and it *was* loving, not just lustful, when my roommate went home one weekend and his best friend came to our dorm for a visit, spent the night, and taught me a thing or two—from that moment, the floodgates were opened, and I soon found myself surrounded by a circle of gay friends. The age of liberation was only dawning, and the lifestyle I learned was guarded, but word of my arrival on the scene traveled fast, as did reports of what I had to offer. Anyone I wanted, I got. And of course I wanted them all.

"On a pizza date one evening with a new friend, I made a discovery about children. My casual disdain for them was transformed to active loathing. We were at a nice place, not the typical campus dive, but a restaurant that specialized in the then-new deep-dish pizza. My friend was old enough to order a pitcher of beer, which we shared. In short, the outing was a treat—nice place, booze, and the promise of adult recreation later. I was feeling very grown-up and loving it.

"Our enchanted evening was interrupted by the entrance of a couple and their child. The kid was three or four, noisy and contrary, a real brat. But he was the apple of mommy and daddy's eye, and he wanted fwench fwies. The waitress explained that they didn't have french fries, only pizza. The child responded with a screaming, kicking tantrum. Daddy got up and headed out the door—I presumed he was going to the car for a muzzle. Mommy tried to mollify her treasure with a kiddy cocktail, which ended up on the floor. The scene climaxed several minutes later when daddy returned with a Double Whammy Burger and a large order of fries, fetched from a joint around the corner. The child dried his tears and began to munch contentedly, but *our* meal had been ruined. Later that night, at the ripe old age of nineteen, I experienced my first-ever bout of indigestion. Never, I vowed, would I sink to the brainlessness of the parents I saw that night.

"My resolution may have seemed a moot gesture, coming from a gay kid with no inclination to marry. But there was a wrinkle.

I had lived since adolescence in fear of being drafted. I don't know whether it stemmed from a survival instinct or simply from my distaste for uniforms, but the prospect of 'serving' was unthinkable, and you needed a deferment to keep out. The obvious solution was to declare myself gay, get branded 4F, and be done with it. But those were closeted times, and friends warned that I shouldn't even consider it. Short of shooting myself in the foot, my options for deferment boiled down to school or marriage.

"I was already in school, but getting antsy, convinced that design wasn't something to study, but something to do. If I was destined—by fate, or my parents, or my own talents—to become a decorator, then I wanted to get on with it and earn a living so I could pursue my theatrical interests on the side. If I quit school, though, I'd be slapped with an induction notice before swagging my first tieback. I was forced to consider marriage.

"There was a girl in the design program at school who was hot for me. She was pretty and stylish. I wasn't interested in her *that* way, but we'd become chummy, often working late together on class projects, laughing up a storm, dishing classmates and teachers alike. As we came to know more about each other, I liked what I learned. She was the daughter, the only child, of the man who owned a big high-end interiors store there in town. It was a place much like Potter's—not, strictly speaking, a design studio, but a glorified furniture store that carried good lines and employed a staff of designers as salesmen. This looked promising, so I let our relationship slide toward the romantic. Our late-night talks turned from the foibles of our classmates to deeper matters. In the most veiled terms, I told her where I was coming from and how difficult marriage might be for me. She assured me she understood. She knew I was 'different' and 'sensitive.' She was content to be that 'special woman' in my life.

"Sold. On a lovely Saturday morning following the last exam of our junior year, we were married. Our families were overjoyed. My friends were dismayed, even sickened by my turnaround. They didn't understand that, in exchange for my reasonable if not absolute fidelity, I was able to quit school, keep my deferment, and go to work for Big Daddy, returning at night to a well-furnished home and a loving wife who had career goals, a sense of humor, and no maternal instincts.

"Or so I thought. By the end of our first year together, she was dropping hints. After two years, we were arguing about it. At the end of the third year, she was pregnant, and during the fourth, the baby arrived. It was a horrible mistake. I may have loved the baby in some abstract, parental sense, but I certainly never liked her. As an infant she was a predictable nuisance, and as a toddler she was worse. My marriage was deteriorating fast, and as it crumbled, so did my working relationship with Big Daddy. The only sane option was to start over. I quit my job, divorced my wife, said good-bye to my daughter, and got the hell out of town.

"My credentials were solid by then, so I had no trouble finding work. I chose Potter's because it's a good shop—and a short drive across the long bridge from Evanstown. While married, I'd enjoyed the lazy sophistication of life in a college town. And the opportunities for theater made Evanstown seem all the more appealing.

"Shortly after I arrived and settled into my job, I got a dog. I suppose he replaced some of the missing parts of my life. He was a magnificent weimaraner, a sleek thoroughbred, a man's dog. I named him Butch. His color was perfect—neither too steely nor too ruddy—an absolutely neutral gray. He inspired a phase in my decorating that set me apart and put me in demand. I came on strong with schemes of gray while every other decorator, from Manhattan to Peoria, was stuck on the beiges. So I owe Butch a lot. Not only was he an affectionate companion, but he sparked the sole design coup of my career.

"Butch died a few years ago, and I buried him under the birdbath behind the house—I'd like to be buried there with him, it's so tranquil and pretty. It was sort of a garden party. I served cocktails to take the focus off death. I never got another dog. Butch had filled a need, but by the time he died, Guy had entered my life.

"I'm surprised I found him. Guy's good for me, rounds me out. He's intellectual and levelheaded. And it doesn't hurt that he's ten years younger. He's built like a gymnast, used to *be* a gymnast, a real turn-on both in and out of bed. That means a lot, now that I'm pushing forty. Sure, I love Guy—as much as I'm capable of loving one man. He's achieving his goals, happy with his career, and settled for life, right here in Evanstown. Sometimes he makes me want to scream.

"Potter's is just a job. I gave up the notion ages ago that there's any glamour to it. Making things worse, I've never liked Nellie Potter—well, his name's Neil—the old queen who owns the store. He treats his gay designers like a stable of courtesans. Nothing overt. It's an air, a posture.

"Thank God for the Evanstown Players. Acting is my truest love. Maybe it points the way out of this trap.

"Theater is your life, Claire. I've said it's mine too, but that was wishful thinking. I'm stuck rehearsing, always getting ready for the next act, the fresh beginning that's just beyond reach. I rehearse in the shower each morning, thinking out loud. If the day ever comes to tell Nellie that I quit, the speech will be a scorcher; I've honed it well. Then there's a sad speech, a delicate one that tells Guy I'm leaving for New York. This evening, too— it was rehearsed. The things I'm telling you now, I've told myself before. Is that so strange? Hey, you awake?"

"Wide awake," she tells me, rolling her head on my shoulder. "No, it's not strange that you rehearse. I don't talk to myself in the shower, but I often find my daily musings surprisingly structured, as if I were telling a story or setting the scene for a play. Perhaps it's a symptom of our theatrical minds to view the world as if through a proscenium, suspending reality, spinning thoughts like lines for a script."

I ponder her words with satisfaction. "Then Doctor Solomon was wrong. He lectured me this morning on reality and fantasy, truth and lies. But he's been dealing, as you say, with a theatrical mind, so of course my reality doesn't fit his scientific view. He was simply wrong."

"Be careful, George. Don't dismiss him too casually. Indulging in fantasy for the sake of art is one thing, but living it is quite another. Maybe that's what he meant."

"I'm touched by your concern," I tell her dryly, "but let's talk about something else. Tell me about your play."

"Hm." She sits up in bed, crossing her legs Indian-style while draping herself with the sheet. "The play relates to what we've been discussing, but it's a bit philosophical." She closes her eyes in thought. "We're talking about reality, George. Your concern, I hope, is to deal with reality in its broadest sense—the world and your role in it. My problem is a narrower kind of reality—the nature of relationships." She opens her eyes and rivets me with a stare. "Still with me?"

"Yes, professor."

She continues, "This has vexed me since childhood. Simply put, my mother made me feel that I was better than other people. It was her way, I suppose, of building my self-esteem—as well as her own. God knows, she needed it. She and my father were estranged from the time I was born. They never divorced or even separated; he just wasn't around much.

"When I grew old enough to understand such things, I got the idea that he was keeping a mistress. I wanted to talk to him about it, but the time was never right. I wasn't upset by the idea; I just wanted to know. Actually, I hope he did have a mistress. He deserved some happiness. He died almost twenty years ago, and I've never discussed this hunch with my mother.

"I don't know whether it was the cause or the result of my father's wandering eye, but my mother has always been a woman of 'attitude.' There's no nice way to say it: She's a snob. And she turned *me* into one too.

"In the countless ways that a mother can influence her child, she taught me to look down on other people. Maybe they had less money or less education. Maybe they went to the wrong church or even the wrong hairdresser. She could always find something to convince me that they were lacking. It's no wonder, then, that I grew up pretty damned pleased with myself. Lonely too. Marriage? Who could possibly fit the bill?

"Even as a child, I had few friends, precocious interests, and a will of iron. Many little girls dream of blossoming into star-lets, but my theatrical goal was different: I would become a director. I had to be the boss. Theater is a risky career for anyone, and directing is especially chancy for a woman. But I have never been afraid of risks, and I've discovered that directing is easy. You tell people what to do, they do it, and everyone is rewarded with bouquets and applause. Life certainly doesn't work that way. People don't always do what they're told, nor should they.

"It's ironic that I owe my success to the ambitions and self-confidence that my mother gave me. By learning to set myself apart from the rest of the world, I've built a life that has been essentially unhappy. And I've accepted this as both necessary and normal.

"There's so much I should never have listened to when I was

young, but I was in no position then to make meaningful judgments. They teach us such crap—and it has colored and twisted every important encounter of my life, from my mother to Hector Bosch, the derelict in the park, and now you. But I'm learning."

"What derelict?"

"Never mind the derelict. The point is that it's time for me to slough off this confusion and face a simple but elusive reality: Adults enter relationships as traders might, expecting to take as well as to give, aware and unashamed that the motive for trade is the taking, not the giving. It's a lesson you've helped teach me tonight, and it's a lesson worth sharing through my play."

As she arrives at this conclusion, I stifle a yawn.

"Hope I'm not boring you," she says. "Tired?"

"All fagged out."

"Poor baby. You've had a trying night."

PART THREE
*U*PSTAGE, *D*OWNSTAGE

G E O R G E

A warm April morning. *Traders* opens in a month. Cutting my hair now, cutting it short, combing my hand through it, snipping the tufts between my fingers. With four weeks' growth, it'll be thick and full, a crown of curls, picture-perfect in the scrapbooks of Evanstown, a lingering memory long after I've left this place.

Seven months have passed since I first slept with Claire. Though a passive partner that night, she assured me she would contribute more actively to future flings. If I doubted her, I shouldn't have. If I felt her age and her sex were guarantees of docility, I was wrong. And if I thought past promiscuities had taught me every trick in the book, I was surprised to learn a few new ones.

After the September rains, during the dry, cool weeks of

October, the sugar maples outside Claire's huge window turned crimson, and Evanstown turned inward. The faculty donned its tweeds, the students cracked their books, and the decorating business boomed as nest-featherers cast critical glances toward the great indoors. Claire was busy writing and teaching; I was busy with work and my Noel Coward role. But we found plenty of time for each other, and our affair, if not quite a romance, took on the character of friendship.

Claire showed surprising interest in my play. After I'd spent several evenings memorizing lines, buried alone in my script, she couldn't resist offering help. This play was kid's stuff to her, but she was gracious and patient, explaining lines that confused me, suggesting new inflections and twists of phrasing. "It's not critical," she told me, "that every script be learned verbatim, but then we're not always dealing with Noel Coward. Suffice it to say, this man could *write*. So we'll pay him the courtesy of leaving his work intact."

And indeed we did, down to the comma. I've never been better prepared for a production, which is fitting, since Claire attended every performance—"just scouting," she said, for the cast of her own play. She congratulated me, as did many others, on a job well done. I began to feel confident I was being groomed for her leading role.

She lent me Kiki's cherished little car and told me to drive it often. I was happy to be entrusted with it, and we took long, late rides together before the nights turned cold.

The view from the huge window turned murky as November slid toward December. Winter's first winds whipped over the Upper Ridge, swirling clouds of dead leaves through the town, dropping them in heaps along the banks of Evans Run. On nights when I slept with Claire, mornings came later and darker. I slipped home beneath the cold glare of streetlights to shower before driving to work.

Guy watched my growing involvement with Claire unemotionally, aware that my motive was ambition, not lust. Finding my affair more amusing than threatening, he never missed a chance to jab me with a bitchy innuendo. I don't know if he tricked on my nights out—he dropped no clues, and I was in no position to pry.

With the approach of Christmas, Claire decided to spend the

holidays at her mother's home in upstate New York, claiming to dread the visit. So we planned a Christmas of our own, a week early after Monday's class. She made a simple steak dinner. "It's not very traditional," she told me, "but I'd ruin a goose, and I've never liked it anyway." Unknown to her, the evening was a double celebration for me, if "celebration" can correctly describe a birthday. I had just turned forty. I wondered during the meal if I would age gracelessly, like so many vapid queens, forever thirty-nine.

After dinner we exchanged gifts. She gave me a book, and I gave her a bottle of champagne, not Dom Pérignon, but the best I could find in Evanstown. I hoped she would open it then and there, but she stowed it in the refrigerator, saying she would keep it for a special occasion. Around midnight, we were startled by the phone. It was Manny. He must have delivered good news because, after Claire hung up, she announced it was time to pop the champagne.

When Claire returned from New York in January, the full force of winter had hit Evanstown. Through the huge window, black branches traced delicate patterns over a thick, unspoiled crust of snow. With the holidays behind them, students and faculty prepared for the last few weeks of the semester. Claire's seminar would soon end, and she offered to let me audit her spring course. I declined, but suggested that I continue my Monday night visits after class. She agreed, and my school days drew to a close.

At the end of the month, semester break, Guy went to Arizona to visit an old friend who had just installed a swimming pool. I stayed behind, since school vacations have no bearing on the furniture business. Claire stayed too. She had reached a critical stage in her writing and needed to work on it undisturbed.

Halfway through the break, she phoned me late on a Saturday. Breathy with excitement, she told me she'd spent an especially productive evening at work on her play. A crucial speech, a long monologue, had been troubling her for weeks but finally fell together that night. She felt like putting her work aside for a day. She wanted to go sledding. "Do you happen to have a toboggan?" she asked. No, but I knew where to get one. Though wary of the whole idea, I agreed to meet her the next morning at the top of a hill that has long been favored for student sledding parties.

Sunday dawned winter-gray under a thick cover of clouds, heavy with snow. There was no wind, so the cold had no bite. It took longer than I'd planned to attach the borrowed toboggan to the roof of the roadster, so I was late arriving to meet Claire. At the top of the hill were several picnic tables, but only one was occupied that morning. Claire had brushed the snow from one of the benches and cleared a spot on the table for a large Thermos. A tree spread its bare branches over her like gnarled, knotty fingers. She sat very still, holding a mug of coffee below her face. Swathed in layers of muted wool, with a long scarf draping past her knees, she was indeed beautiful in that serene setting.

She had seen me drive up and watched me remove the toboggan from the car, but made no move to greet me. When I dragged the sled in her direction, she raised a single gloved finger to her lips. There on the ground, only inches from her feet, a pair of tiny birds—wrens, perhaps, or chickadees—pecked in the snow at morsels of something that had dropped from the tree. I approached as quietly as I could, but when I drew too near, they chirped and fluttered away. Claire rose with a smile, we kissed hello, and she offered me her coffee. I slurped a few mouthfuls. Wagging a mitten at the long sled, I told her, "This thing looks tricky. Dangerous, too—look down that hill."

"Now, George. I admit I'm a bit eccentric, and I often find risk alluring, but I'm no fool. Do you think I'd be here, at my age, if there were any real danger? There's nothing 'tricky' about it. Just get on the sled and slide down the damn hill. I'll sit in front and steer; you sit in back and wrap your legs around me."

She was right. It couldn't have been simpler, and it was fun. We streaked down the hill again and again, taking turns sitting in front. A light snow began to sift through the branches above. Our laughter turned to screams as we veered ever closer to the tree trunks blurring past us. Each time we trudged back up the hill, we warmed ourselves with more coffee from the Thermos. After an hour or two, it was empty.

"I don't know about you," she told me, "but I'm worn out."

"I don't know about *you*," I retorted, shaking the Thermos before her, "but I've got to pee so bad I can taste it."

"Ditto. Let's go home and build a fire."

We wasted no time loading the car and speeding back to

Claire's house. "I'd laugh about this," she told me as we bolted through the door, "but it hurts."

Soon, we did laugh about it. While I lit the fire, she concocted an après-toboggan drink, remembered from her student days. Consisting of brandy and God-knows-what, it had to be boiled, then drunk with a cinnamon stick. I find all such drinks—glogg, grog, toddies, mulled wine—equally disgusting. For the sake of her nostalgia trip, though, I raised a mug of the steaming swill. After two sips, she declared her brew unpalatable and dumped the potful. It swirled down the drain with a belch of protest from the plumbing.

I suggested that we slip into the matching pair of robes she brought back from her Christmas trip to New York. We could get cozy by the fire with something not warm, but cold—a Ramos fizz. "Marvelous idea," she agreed with a playful grin, and we changed into our robes. While she mounded a nest of cushions before the fire, I blended our batch of drinks, delivering them on a tray. We toasted and drank.

We lounged among the pillows, gazing past the fire at the wintry scene beyond the huge window, savoring the contrast of ice and flames. The snow was falling harder now, and the wind was picking up. We laughed at the approaching storm and made another batch of fizzes. She read me the all-important speech she'd written the night before. I listened quietly, but found it incomprehensible—due, no doubt, to the liquor. I told her it was fabulous. After another batch of fizzes, when the gin ran out, we staggered from the pillows to the bed. The storm howled, the fire hissed, and the sky grew darker.

We had sex. Even in her stupor, Claire insisted, as always, that I use the condom she provided. When I made an offhand crack about safe sex, she said, "Plenty safe for you. The risk is all mine."

The view from the huge window didn't change much during the next two months, but sometime in February, Claire finished her play. In an intimate way, I shared her accomplishment, her high. And the joy I felt was not mere empathy. A role now awaited me that could change my life.

Out of the blue, Claire told me one night as we lay in her bed, "It's good, George. The play—it works. It turned out better than I dared hope."

"Does that mean you've decided? You'll direct *Traders* here in

Evanstown this spring?"

"Damn right, kiddo. And unless I'm sorely mistaken, they're going to love it at home."

She was referring, of course, to Broadway. I kissed her, then slept. I dreamed the sweet nothings of a baby that night.

In late March, when the view from the huge window hinted of spring, Claire cast her play. The process lasted a week, with general tryouts followed by two callback sessions. During this period, we suspended my overnight visits.

Monday's general tryouts drew actors and actresses from both the college and the Evanstown Players. I was surprised to see several high schoolers and a few out-of-towners auditioning as well. Only six roles would be awarded, and the odds made me nervous. Claire and her stage manager, seated at the center of the auditorium, took notes and shuffled résumés while we recited our prepared readings. Then we read dialogue from the script in round-robin sequence with each other.

After three hours of this, she rose and told us, "Thank you, everyone. I appreciate your patience. I'm impressed by what I've heard; now I face some difficult decisions. Callbacks will be announced Wednesday at noon. Watch the board outside the department office." She closed her book and gathered her papers, signaling that we could leave.

As we filed out of the auditorium, she called after me, "Mr. McBeth?" and summoned me with a wag of her finger. "I see on your résumé that you're employed at Potter's. That's out of town, isn't it? You needn't waste your lunch hour checking the call-board. I'll tell you now: Yes, you will be called back. Be here Wednesday night, please. Seven sharp."

Wednesday's callbacks went well. So did Thursday's. I was clearly in the running for the lead role, but it wasn't clinched. Claire would post the cast tomorrow at noon. She made no offer to save me the midday drive from Potter's, so I was left in suspense with the others.

I slept terribly that night and was a basket case at work Friday morning. I sneaked out early for lunch and drove to the campus with a shaky hand on the wheel and a heavy foot on the gas. I walked through the halls toward the theater office, dazed. A girl passed me in tears. Christ, the call-board lay dead ahead. Centered on it was the freshly typed list. I stepped up to it not daring, at first, to look. Then I opened my eyes to peek at the top of the page. I blinked, staring at my name for a moment. "My God!" I shouted for the benefit of anyone within earshot. "I got it!"

Rehearsals began that night with a read-through. It was eight weeks till opening, a long rehearsal schedule because Claire expected there'd be script changes. Two weeks would be for blocking. During the third week, we'd have a run-through. After four, lines would be due—no scripts onstage.

That was four weeks ago; lines are due tonight. I know them, but I'm nervous this morning, scared I'll choke. There's a lump in my throat that won't go away. I'm cutting my hair. Cutting it short so it'll be perfect on opening night. Watching it drift in wisps to the bathroom floor. Room's a mess. *I'm* a mess. Can't go like this. Have to shower.

"No, not again." Already running late, but have to wash. Made an appointment with Doctor Solomon. Haven't seen the bastard since he dumped me last fall, but need to see him now. Stuck in the shower, running my lines, running late, washing my hair away. Washing myself, touching myself.

"Not now!" Need to get out of here, need some reassurance. Xanax, maybe. Get a grip on things. "Save it, damn it." Let go of it. Wash it. Has to be clean, squeaky clean, so clean that it hurts. Washing, washing like the lady from Shakespeare.

"Got to get a grip on things." Choking. Rehearsing.

As I rush past Solomon's receptionist and through the door to the doctor's inner office, he looks up from behind his desk and asks, "What happened to your hair?"

My fingers dart to my scalp. "I guess it got mussed on the way over. I've been driving Kiki's roadster, and I had the top down. Beautiful day, huh? Looks like spring has sprung."

"George," he says with a troubled voice, motioning for me to sit, "you haven't been here since September. You phoned for an appointment, complaining of acute anxiety, sounding fairly desperate. You arrive with your hair chopped off, looking—if I might say so—like hell. Now you tell me, 'Spring has sprung.' Are you really here to talk about the weather?"

"*Excuse* the small talk," I tell him, indignant, while planting myself in the chair. "Excuse my appearance, too. I'm working on a play, in case you haven't heard. It opens in a month, and this 'look' is essential to my role. That's why I'm here—not the weather, not my hair, but the play."

"Terrific," he says, dismissing my moodiness. "I'm dying to hear about it. Whole town's curious. Judging from your hair, I'd guess the play must be set in a prison camp."

"It happens to be set in a little town that reminds Claire of the place where she went to school. Get it? She told me once that Evanstown reminds her of *Our Town*, and it turns out that her play is sort of like *Our Town*, except not so folksy. Not so plotty, either. It's abstract, philosophical. There are only six characters. For example: Jerome, the character I'm playing, has some problems."

"What sort of problems?" he asks while jotting something on his pad.

"Jerome's not screwy or anything"—I whirl a finger at my temple—"but he's gay, and he's confused. In the end, he gets his head together."

"What's he confused about? Be specific."

"The usual bag of dilemmas. Goals, career, sex."

"Most people don't see these issues as dilemmas, George. Certainly, confronting the basic decisions of life can be scary. Hurdles frighten us. But adults learn to confront these issues, make decisions, and cross the hurdles. It's part of growing up. How old are you now? Forty, forty-one?"

"Thirty-nine."

"Close enough. Point is, most of us—at our age—come to grips with reality and learn that the junctures of life are simply turning points, not endless brick walls of confusion."

"I find that hard to believe, doctor. After all, Jerome is confused by life's dilemmas. So am I."

"Then you should be well suited for the role. It sounds tailor-made for you."

I shrug my shoulders.

He continues, "By the end of the play, Jerome's got his head together. How does he do it?"

"Lots of talk. This script contains the longest speech I've ever memorized. Jerome shares an important scene with another character, a woman he's been intimate with—like I said, he's gay, but mixed up. She says to him, 'I know many things *about* you,

Jerome, but I don't really *know* you. Tell me about yourself.'
That's my cue. I launch into a slow, rambling monologue that
covers everything from Jerome's childhood to his current state of
mind. At first he's talking to the other character, but he soon
forgets she's there. The lighting isolates him as he moves
downstage, speaking directly to the audience. Claire tells me to
think of the proscenium as the frame of a giant mirror. I'm
looking at my own reflection, thinking out loud."

"Stream of consciousness—whatever comes to mind."

"Exactly. It's effective theater."

"It can also be effective analysis. I'm curious—how does
Jerome wrap up this soliloquy?"

"You'll love this; it reminds me of our discussion, last time I
was here. Jerome glides into the old song-and-dance about reality
and fantasy. Particularly, the reality of relationships. He's on a
guilt trip because he's used people, and his expectations have
been way out of line."

"That must be a profound realization for him. I assume Claire
considers the scene pivotal?"

"Pivotal? She told me point-blank that this scene is the heart
of the play. We rehearse it again and again, and she always asks
if I understand it, and I tell her, sure, the words seem plain
enough. Then, just when I'm convinced I have it perfect, we start
over. I come to every rehearsal half an hour before the others so
we can work on it. It's weird how she hammers away at that
speech."

Solomon looks me in the eye. "Perhaps Claire sees parallels
between you and Jerome. Through her emphasis of this scene,
couldn't she be trying to tell you something?"

I explain to him, "Claire Gray is one of the world's great
directors. She's a perfectionist. She's hammering at that scene
because it's important to her play. If she wanted to tell me
something, she'd simply tell me. This may come as a shock to
you, doctor, but Claire and I have had ample time for idle chatter.
We've been sleeping together."

"This may come as a shock to *you*, George, but your little affair
is hardly a secret. The town's buzzing."

I laugh off his words. "Come on, Solomon—no bullshit,
okay? You're toying with a tortured mind." I slouch in my
chair, raising a limp hand to my forehead.

"I'm not toying with you." His tone is flat, tinged with neither humor nor rancor. "Everyone is well aware of your affair with Claire Gray."

"That's impossible. We've been so discreet, so careful."

"Face facts, George. This is a small town, Claire is a celebrity, and you've always been something of a notorious character yourself. Do you honestly think, after sleeping with this woman for half a year, that nobody knows about it? The way I hear it, when you took the seminar at her house last fall, you always stayed after class. People were talking the first night."

"All right, people know. So what? A little scandal's good for this town, shakes the cobwebs out of some dusty, small minds. Besides, who cares what people think? I got the part, didn't I? That's what matters."

"And how has Guy reacted to all this?"

"He thinks it's great. He's behind me a hundred percent."

"If everything's rosy, why are you here?"

"Rehearsal tonight—lines are due. We've had a month to memorize our parts, but now we're off-book, and I'm a *wreck* over it. All the old anxiety symptoms are back. I've been hyper-ventilating, I'm aware of my pulse, and the lump in my throat is bugging me again. I'm afraid I'll choke tonight."

"But why, George? You're an experienced actor."

"This role is different," I explain with growing impatience. "Not only does my future hang on it, but it contains the longest speech I've ever tried to learn."

"If you flub the speech at rehearsal, what happens?"

"I stop and call out, 'Line.' The stage manager feeds me the next few words."

"In other words, it doesn't matter if you screw up your lines tonight, and you've got a month left to perfect them. Seriously," he tells me, raising his brows in an expression of frankness, "this doesn't strike me as cause for an attack."

"But *I'm* the one with symptoms," I remind him. "I've been through this before, and I recognize what's happening."

He leans forward, elbows on the desk, hands folded. He asks quietly, "Then how do we deal with this problem?"

My gaze has been darting around the room—from the wall of diplomas to the shelves of books, the Manila folder that contains my file, the clock that says my time is nearly up—but now I fix my eyes on his as I suggest, "Tranks."

"I don't know," he says, more to himself than to me. "Sure, I could prescribe tranquilizers to calm you down and get you over the hump, but that wouldn't really solve anything, and it might create new problems. If your prime concern is your acting, you'll need full control of your wits. There's nothing I can give you that won't have dulling side effects. I don't know, George."

Barely above a whisper, I ask, "Please?"

He hesitates, then pulls a pad from his desk drawer and begins to write. "Very well. Xanax, little bitty ones, point-two-five milligrams. No refills." He rips the sheet from the pad and hands it to me with the warning, "Don't overdo it."

"Thank you, doctor," I tell him while glancing over the prescription. "This ought to do the trick. I'll get it filled, go home, and work on lines—have to be in top form at tonight's rehearsal."

"What about your job? Aren't you supposed to be at work?"

"I phoned in sick."

He eyes me with a smirk.

"I had a doctor's appointment, didn't I? Besides, I don't give a rat's ass about Potter's. Another month or so, and I'll be ready to kiss that place good-bye." I stare at him with a broad smile, relishing the imminent demise of my decorating career.

He meets my stare with a blank gaze, then asks, very softly, "You think so?"

"I know so, Solomon. It's part of the plan."

There's something smug about the way he says, "The only thing left, then, is to wish you good luck."

"Wrong," I correct him as I fold the prescription and slip it into my pocket. "You shouldn't tell an actor that. It's considered bad luck. You're supposed to say, 'Break a leg.'"

As I rise from the chair and turn to leave, he flips my file closed and says, "Good luck, George."

I normally arrive at rehearsals with no time to spare, having dawdled and fussed before leaving the house—changing clothes, running my lines, maybe a quick shower—but tonight I'm early. I am calm.

Entering the theater from its lobby, I see Claire seated at her makeshift desk in the fifth row of seats. She works beneath the glare of a battered typing lamp, scrawling notes on a stack of three-by-five cards. The stage is bare except for a few folding chairs and a work light that casts long, harsh shadows.

I bound down the aisle, announcing my arrival with a cheery "Good evening, Claire."

She looks over her shoulder. Her smile fades to a squint as I draw near, and then she screams. Her yelp reverberates in the empty hall as she covers her mouth with her hand. "Your hair!" she gasps through splayed fingers. "What the hell happened to your hair?"

I drop into the seat next to hers and explain with a shrug, "I cut it."

"You cut it *yourself?*" she asks, recoiling from me. "It looks as if you were bound, gagged, and ritually shorn by some cult sadist." Her eyes haven't left the top of my head. She sighs, then whimpers, "But why, George?"

Unsure of my answer, I stammer, "Well, it was getting long, and the weather's getting warm, and . . . "

"But, honey, why so short?" She extends a cautious hand to tug at one of my newly trimmed locks, coaxing it to grow. "It'll never fill out by opening night."

"Sure it will," I tell her with a confident laugh. "It grows so fast, it'll be fine in a month."

"Hm," she snorts, unconvinced, then adds in a lecturing tone, "My characters are bigger than life, and I want them to appear that way. If your hair hasn't grown back in time"—she wags a finger in my face—"you'll be wearing a wig!"

She straightens her stack of notes and continues, "Let's get down to business. Lines are due tonight. Can you try your scene without the script?"

"I'm ready," I tell her. "But I might stumble—nerves, you know."

She puts down her cards, peers at me, and pats my hand. "Fine, darling, no need to be nervous. There's a month to go." She looks into my eyes for a moment, then says, "I assumed it was only your hair, George, but you seem 'different' tonight." She leans close to ask, "Have you been drinking?" While waiting for my answer, her nostrils flare to sniff my breath.

"Of course not," I tell her. "I haven't had a drink all day." Changing the subject, I suggest, "Let's get to work."

"Yes, let's. But not the whole scene—only the ending, the soliloquy. Places, please?"

I rise from my seat and make a deliberate gesture of leaving my script on the cushion. I trot down the aisle and climb the stairs at the apron of the stage. I find my position, then close my eyes, slipping into the character of Jerome.

Claire sets the scene: "You've completed the long opening of the monologue, telling us of your boyhood, your awakening sexuality, and the confusion that plagues your relationships. You've stepped downstage to think, to sort things out. Your face and hands glow in the thin beam of a pencil-spot. Jerome is alone. He's picking away at something—very carefully, the way he'd pick at a scab—and he's afraid he'll bleed if he picks too fast. But he won't bleed. In the end, he'll make a discovery that can change his life."

She pauses. "Now, take it from 'Got to get a grip on things.'"

Eyes closed, I nod slowly, implying that I understand what she wants. But I don't. We've been over this so often, and she keeps digging deeper. Got to get a grip on things. The words stick in my throat. Seconds pass. Starting to sweat.

She says, "Whenever you're ready . . . "

"Sorry, Claire," I blurt at her. "I don't know what to do with my hands."

"Forget your hands," she tells me with an edge of impatience. "Sit on them if you must. Tonight I want to work on interpretation, so please—say the words."

Got to get a grip on things. I shove my hands into my pockets. Deep breath. Do it.

"Got to get a grip on things." The sound of my voice triggers a mechanism, jogs my memory, and the speech begins to flow. "Time to look around me. Time to see things as they really are." Familiar words, Jerome's words, Claire's, not mine. But I bring them to life, claiming them as my own. I see the spotlight. Though not yet lit, it will shine on my face, mine alone in the darkness of the hall. And I hear my voice, mine alone that breaks the stillness. Out there, a crowd of faces stares and listens, hanging on every word, guided by every nuance, swayed by the flick of an eyelid, the furrow of my brow, the tension mounting in my thighs. They gaze at me as if upon an athlete, shameless and indulgent. They've paid the price, surrendered their tickets, and come to gawk. I see only what they see—myself, in a mirror, alone and aroused. I hear only what they hear. The words flow faster, a torrent now. Claire's words, Doctor Solomon's, not mine. Words and more words—inane or profound?—a grist of words for the actor's mill. Memorize, repeat. Interpret, repeat. Say it over, get it right, letter-perfect.

The speech is finished. The lighting fades up as Jerome turns to discover the character forgotten in the shadows. I deliver the next line: "Don't you see?"

"Not bad."

At the sound of Claire's voice, my eyes dart toward the audience. She is no longer seated at the director's table, but at the edge of the stage. Surprised to find her so near, I tell her, "I didn't see you move."

"I know you didn't. That's good. You were wrapped up in your scene." She pats the stage floor. "Come sit by me."

I sit at her side, shoulder to shoulder.

She says, "I think you were beginning to feel it. Getting rid of the script did wonders for your delivery. But there's a lot of work ahead of us."

"The hard part's over," I tell her. "I've got my lines. I made it through without a flub." Smiling at her, proud of myself, I expect a smile in return, maybe a compliment.

But there's a touch of sadness in the way she tells me, "Acting is more than memorizing lines, honey. You have to feel their meaning. Are you beginning to feel what Jerome feels? In your *own* mind, have we pared away the gristle, the scrap, and gotten down to the meat of that speech?"

"Sure, Claire. The words seem plain enough. I see exactly what you're driving at."

I don't know what the hell she's talking about.

PART FOUR
TRADERS

C   L   A   I   R   E

Wrenching *Traders* from my head and committing it to paper took six months. It was a creative, introspective period, nicely spiced by my exploits with George. The two months of rehearsal, by contrast, were hectic and anxiety-ridden. Occupied by the usual concerns of a director, I was also haunted by the insecurities of a playwright, never allowing a rehearsal to pass without tinkering with the script. When opening night finally arrived last week, I greeted the event with mixed and charged emotions. On the one hand, the period of labor had ended; on the other, my work would now be judged.

If it failed, news would spread instantly. Seated in the audience was a host of critics, not only from the college paper and from the Evanstown *Courier*, but from many out-of-town publications, including the New York *Weekly Review*. For the first time, I found myself fearing Hector Bosch's unmatched stature as an opinionator. Past intimacies would not compromise his professionalism if he were disappointed by *Traders*.

Adding to my jitters, Hector brought Arnold Manley as a guest that night. Publicity for his movie, *Inner Moments*, had made Manny an overnight celebrity, and his presence lent an aura of Hollywood to my premiere. The governor of Massachusetts was there too, but his entrance was totally upstaged by Manny's appearance.

Suffice it to say, last Friday was the most tension-filled evening of my career. My worst concern, however, had nothing to do with my script. *Traders* was in fact a great success. Hector proclaimed, with his voice of self-fulfilling prophecy, that it will be a long-running Broadway smash. And Manny can't wait to begin rehearsals. So the problem wasn't the play. No, the problem was George.

A few minutes before curtain, I went backstage to talk to the cast. This theatrical tradition, akin to a locker-room pep talk, is especially productive with amateur actors. I found my players in darkened corners of the wings. Without being summoned, they looked up from their thoughts and gathered around me. My red dress drew several wolfish comments, pleasing me immensely.

"We've worked hard for eight weeks," I told them, "and tonight, it all comes together onstage. You're giving birth to a play—every line you utter will breathe life into it—but ultimately, you're creating a new reality. And when you succeed at extracting reality from illusion, your craft has become art."

I paused for a long beat while my words sank in, then added, "You *are* artists. You've proven yourselves by helping me finish *Traders*. Now I'm convinced that the play is ready. And you too are ready. Spend these remaining minutes getting into character. Think of where we've been together, and think of where we're going."

As I said this, George winked at me. It was neither a gesture of affirmation nor an innocent expression of comradery. His wink was slow, deliberate, conspiratorial.

Losing my train of thought, I concluded by asking the group, "Any questions before we begin?"

A girl in the cast, the youngest, asked in a gushy tone, "Is it true, Miss Gray, about *who's* out there? Rumors are flying backstage that *he's* in the audience."

Deducing that the young lady had little interest in the governor and even less in Hector Bosch, I conceded, "If you're referring to Arnold Manley, yes, he's in the house tonight."

The girl's eyes turned heavenward, her shoulders slumped, and she breathed a tiny sigh. Her rapture proved infectious, and the rest of the cast began babbling about Arnold Manley.

Quashing their excitement, I rapped my hands like a disapproving schoolmarm. "Now people, people. We have a play to perform. Nothing beyond the proscenium need concern you. Besides—as far as celebrities go—*you're* the stars tonight."

It was, I confess, an insipid thing to say, but it produced the intended effect, calming the cast and bolstering their confidence. As if with an audible click, they switched their minds to their acting. The girl closed her eyes in contemplation. George bit his lower lip white.

"Good," I said softly. "Let's take our places—you onstage, me out front. This evening, I'm just another theatergoer. I've got my red dress on, and I expect to be entertained." We exchanged warm glances. "Now break a leg."

The cast began drifting toward the stage. As George turned to go, I noticed his lip still pinched in his teeth.

"One little thing, George," I called after him, pretending to be concerned about his makeup. "That furrow line looks a tad heavy." I wetted my thumb and dabbed at the pencil mark on his forehead. "Is everything okay? You seem preoccupied."

"Just getting into character."

"I was afraid you might be cowed by having Manny in the audience."

"Manny?"

"Yes, dear. Arnold Manley."

George cocked his head and squinted at me. He asked haltingly, "You mean Manny, the person on the phone, was—is—Arnold Manley?"

"Of course," I told him. "He hates the name Arnold, so I've always called him Manny. Who did you think it was?"

"I wasn't sure. Maybe an agent." He paused, then looked me in the eye to ask, "The night of our Christmas dinner, when he called—why did you open the champagne afterward?"

The weight of his question wasn't clear to me. I stifled a

confused laugh as I answered, "I was celebrating. I'd written Manny to ask if he had any qualms about playing a homosexual, and he phoned to assure me he'd play any role I wrote for him. So if *Traders* goes to New York . . . "

I stopped short, seeing in George's face the effect of my words. His vacant gaze and dumbly parted lips were the picture of shock and dejection. In the same instant, I realized why.

I should have guessed earlier where George's expectations led. He'd dropped enough clues, but I was so immersed in my writing, I was aware of only his most transparent motives. While it was clear from the start that he wanted to play my leading role in Evanstown, it never crossed my mind that he expected me to cast him on Broadway.

I rested against a table behind me, gripping its edge with both hands, exhaling a long sigh. I didn't know what to say, but was certain that the success or failure of *Traders* suddenly hinged not so much on the worth of my script as on the abysmal mood of the actor who stood before me.

"George," I began, "I assumed you knew about Manny, about New York. Wasn't it common knowledge? Good Lord, Hector Bosch didn't waste any time spreading the word in his column."

Even as I mentioned Hector, I recalled the silly mystery of the purloined review. George never read the single sentence that would have squelched his unrealistic ambitions.

The stage manager, who was watching us from the wings, now approached with reticent steps. Tapping his watch, he asked, "Are we ready, Miss Gray? It's eight o'clock."

"Hold the curtain the usual five minutes, then go. You give the cue; I'll be out front." I spoke my orders calmly, conveying the message that nothing was wrong. The stage manager scurried off to his post.

Turning to George, I took his hand and told him, "I guess this isn't what you had in mind. Perhaps I've misled you, but I never meant to. Truly, George—you *may* find yourself on Broadway someday, but I'm afraid it'll take longer than you dreamed. In any event, we've got a play to premiere, and tonight, you're my star."

I fell silent and looked into his eyes, finally coaxing him to smile. I kissed his lips, then he turned and walked to the stage.

I couldn't have known that I would never touch him again, but the emptiness of our kiss filled me with fear and longing. I rushed to the lobby and down the aisle to my seat, brushing a tear from my lash as I watched the houselights fade to black.

After *Traders* closed its brief but triumphant two-night run last Saturday, I slept more soundly than I had in weeks. Sunday, Commencement Day, dawned bright and warm under an azure sky. I rose early to dress for the exercises, as I had done on just such a morning more than a generation ago.

I wore white. Every year since the first graduates left Evans, all the women of the school, students and faculty alike, have worn white on Commencement Day—flowing dresses and big-brimmed hats with satin ribbons. Many alumnae treasure these dresses for a lifetime. Others pass them along to daughters to wear at their own graduations. I'd like to claim I wore the same dress last Sunday that I wore thirty years ago, but I dyed that one red shortly after leaving school, and it long since disappeared.

Exercises are held on the quad. The rear portico of Evans Hall, festooned with flowers, is used as a stage, with the audience seated in the open on white wooden chairs. To the best of my knowledge, the weather has never dampened this tradition, and I've never heard that alternate plans exist.

A more recent tradition dates from the turn of the century, when a student's father, a Navy admiral stationed in Japan, acquired for the college a fabulous collection of paper lanterns. Every year since, in the early-morning hours of Commencement Day, under the supervision of the school's museum curator, a crew of students has unpacked the lanterns and hung them from the fruit trees that dot the quad.

When graduates and their families arrive, an exotic, playful scene greets them and taunts the senses: the fragrance of trees in blossom, the colorful riot of lanterns dancing in the wind, the jangle of slender glass chimes swaying beneath them. Add to this the rustle and swirl of hundreds of white dresses, and the effect is spellbinding. Few designers for the stage could contrive such a setting.

Last Sunday I watched the exercises from two new perspectives—the emotional perspective of my thirty-year absence and the optical perspective of sitting with the faculty instead of the students. But one detail remained the same. Kiki was at my side, wearing the same Evans "uniform." On the morning we graduated, we sat with our fingers linked during the ceremony. Once again I took her hand. We exchanged a quiet smile that spanned the years, listening to the speeches, hearing not a word. A breeze sang softly through the chimes above. The fond memories and festive atmosphere almost made me forget the rising consternation I felt for George.

I hadn't spoken to him since our conversation backstage on opening night. I saw both performances, and through his role, George spoke to me. But try as I might to read between the lines I myself had written, I was unable to penetrate the barrier of the proscenium, to defeat the aesthetic distance that gaped between us, and to know the true state of his mind.

George's acting was sound, mature, and thoroughly competent, but a certain spark was missing from it. Granted, he knew his lines verbatim, never dropped a cue, and took direction precisely. I could suggest a cadence or a shift of inflection, and he fed it back effortlessly. He did everything I asked, but he seemed unable to bring anything of himself to the role. I worked and worked with him on one speech in particular, dissecting every sentence, hoping to share the insights I had gleaned from writing it. Though he read the speech beautifully, I never felt he understood it.

Manny understood it. I could tell from his enthusiasm when he asked for the script. When a role is right for Manny, he feels his lines with rock-solid conviction. He truly becomes the character he portrays, and this is exactly where George's acting fell short.

Poor George, creator and victim of his own delusions. I think of him now with such mixed emotions. He tried to use me, even warned me he was doing it, and I let it happen because I, in turn, used him. I needed him onstage and, yes, I wanted him in bed. The night we first slept together, the night we seduced each other, I was passive as wax. But I knew what I wanted, and we made the exchange. We acted as traders.

Except, I didn't fully know what George was after. Had I known that he expected me to cast him on Broadway, what would I have done? Would I have had the courage to tell him that he will never be the actor Arnold Manley is?

How could he be so naive, so unaware that his role was written for another actor? Gossip travels fast in Evanstown. From the day I arrived, I was quizzed about Manny. Was George so out of touch that he couldn't figure out what everyone else had found obvious? Perhaps the gossip itself shielded him from the truth— not gossip about Manny, but about George and me.

During our weeks of rehearsal, the cast often met afterward for drinks or a late meal, but George never joined them. When I asked him why, he said that things were simply better that way. He was especially sensitive to the issue one day after he saw his psychiatrist. George had learned there was a rumor going around that he and I were sleeping together. I laughed and pointed out that we were indeed sleeping together, to which he mumbled something about small towns and reputations. "Whose reputation are you concerned about," I asked snidely, "*my* reputation as a director, or *your* reputation as a homosexual?" He ended the discussion abruptly with a colorful reference to my vagina.

I don't think I ever came to love George, and I'm certain he never loved me, but we developed a deep affection that went well beyond the bonding of casual sex. Our affair had an edge of secrecy and a spirit of gaming that we both embraced with zest. We had fun. How many lovers, more sincerely impassioned, can claim as much?

On opening night, when George at last realized he would not be going to New York, I felt empathically the anguish of a friend. In the many months we had known each other, it was the first time I really understood him. He sank into a depression that verged—need I say it?—on the suicidal. I felt it. And I was afraid.

Now we needed to talk. I wanted to thank him for the fine job he'd done in *Traders*, to offer some encouraging words about the career he dreamed of. I'd wanted to corner him at the cast party Saturday night and explain how I shared his pain. I wanted to take him aside and suggest that his depression was a process of healing. And I wanted to say good-bye; I was returning to New York on Monday.

But George's absence from the cast party was conspicuous to many and ominous to me. He was, after all, the star of the show, and the show was a great success. I'd hoped his lover, Guy Anderson, might also be there. I wanted to tell him that I knew I was leaving our friend in good hands. And I wanted some assurance that George's ego would soon be on the mend.

I was roused from my thoughts when Kiki slipped her fingers from my grasp and began to clap. I blinked, bemused, and started clapping with the others. When Kiki nudged me with her elbow, I realized that the applause was directed at me, that President Henry had complimented me from the podium. The clapping swelled, so I stood to acknowledge the tribute, bowing first toward the podium, then toward the graduates and guests, and finally toward the faculty seated behind me.

To my surprise, I saw Guy. It hadn't occurred to me that he would attend the exercises, but there he was, seated with the male faculty in the rows behind the women. As my eyes swept the crowd, I fixed my glance on him as if to say, Wait for me afterward, we need to talk.

He smiled, but so did all the others. His stare revealed no panic. He seemed calm. If he harbored no urgent concerns for George, I reasoned that I needn't either, so I sat again facing the podium, waiting for the speeches to end.

But it seemed they would never end. And when they did, the diplomas were awarded—individually. Then a fool in black delivered an embarrassing benediction, exhorting the graduates to pursue lives of self-sacrifice and saintly denial.

The waning spring morning had turned hot and noonish. I fidgeted, palms clammy, anxious for the final Amen. Kiki, sensing my agitation, gave me a wink and patted my hand.

At last it was over. Happy gabbing broke out everywhere as the crowd rose and rushed to mingle. Determined to talk to Guy, I spotted him among the milling faces and tried stepping in his direction, only to find myself trapped by a circle of my own well-wishers.

The guest speakers wanted to meet me, and we were introduced by President Henry. Connie Garamond joked that she would miss being my boss, and her husband, Paul, promised to send me the script of *Magnum Opus* when it was finished. Others delivered messages of congratulations or farewell. And I was cornered by the parents of a student who'd appeared in *Traders*, discussing their daughter's career possibilities.

Throughout these conversations—the interruptions, the hellos, nods, and smiles—I kept turning to locate Guy in the crowd, wanting to know that he would wait, that we would talk. During one stolen glance, he returned my gaze. During another, he

checked his watch. He was moving away from me. I felt the first
dull throb of a headache as I listened to the girl's parents, advis-
ing them vaguely. While I tried to keep track of Guy, the parents
yammered, probing deeper, as though I knew the answers to their
impossible questions. The breeze toyed with the brim of my hat,
crushing my hair beneath it, grinding it into my scalp. The crowd
was dispersing, but their babble grew more boisterous and crude.
A folding chair clapped angrily to the ground. At last the parents
thanked me, and I was free.

But Guy had gone.

I ambled away from the quad as the museum crew arrived with
their ladders to pack away the lanterns till next year.

Tuesday I was home in New York. I returned by train on
Monday, spent the night in my own bed, and awoke refreshed,
as if my experiences in Evanstown had been the vaporous stuff
of a long, disjointed dream. The familiarity of old surroundings
helped me muster my thoughts and tame my emotions. It was
good to be home.

The phone began ringing early. There were calls from friends
who welcomed me back, others regarding production of *Traders*.
My mother phoned twice—once to make sure I arrived safely,
once again to say she'd read that the leading character of my play
was homosexual. She disapproved, suggesting I consider a quick
marriage because "people might talk."

Her calls always upset me, but I was determined not to let her
spoil my mood. It was a pretty spring day, and I wanted to take
a walk through Central Park, perhaps even rent a horse at the
stable. But Central Park reminded me of the Ramble, and my
thoughts were suddenly monopolized by George—his dreams,
his delusions, his uncertain future—and my memory of his
nakedness.

I had to stop. Clear my mind. I couldn't let myself be
consumed by wondering. I would phone him that afternoon.

Arnold Manley was with me; we planned to spend the
morning discussing his new role. He arrived with a pound of
finest Jamaican coffee beans, guessing that my cupboard might
be bare. I ground and brewed some, and we shared quiet
conversation while the caffeine took effect. He also brought a

copy of Monday's *Weekly Review*, containing Hector's critique of my play:

CLAIRE GRAY TRIUMPHS IN EVANSTOWN
'Traders' Broadway-Bound
By Hector Bosch
Senior Critic-at-Large

In the remote foothills of Massachusetts, Claire Gray has cloistered herself for nearly a year on a mission of mercy to lovers of theater. I am happy to report that her efforts have not been in vain. She has developed a wholly new facet of her already illustrious career. Claire Gray has become a playwright. *Traders* opened Friday night at Evans College, and we who saw it were overwhelmed.

It is the story of Jerome, a psychodrama, a struggle to grasp the meaning of human relationships. The principal character is gay, but the play is not about gay issues or homosexuality per se. Jerome's problems are universal, but they are focused and magnified through the anamorphic lens of his sexuality. It is intriguing to ponder how the public will react to Arnold Manley in this role.

Settings are minimal. Costumes are simple and contemporary, except during fantasy sequences when Jerome dons elaborate, erotic garb suggestive of many historical periods, giving the audience brief and sometimes baffling glimpses into the deeper levels of this complex character's psychosexual makeup.

Regular readers are well aware that this writer is seldom at a loss for words . . .

My eye then skipped to the bottom of the article where a name jumped off the page at me:

George McBeth played Jerome, delivering a capable performance with excellent diction and precise timing. A local actor (the cast was entirely amateur), Mr. McBeth rose commendably to his once-in-a-lifetime opportunity to work with a director of Claire Gray's stature. He can proudly remember the role as the highlight of his acting career.

Arnold Manley, who was in the audience on opening night, will surely deliver a more profound theatrical experience than was possible with the local resources in Evanstown, when he brings the starring role to Broadway—as was predicted in this column.

But the true star of this triumph is none other than Claire Gray, for without her expressive talents and depth of ideas, *Traders* would not have been written, and we would all be the poorer.

Brava, dear lady! Hector Bosch has spoken.

Finishing the column, I looked from the paper to Manny, who was speaking to me. Having lost the flow of our conversation, I smiled vacantly and nodded.

Suffice it to say, I was thrilled that Hector pronounced my play an unqualified success, but I dreaded what effect his review might have on George, who'd convinced himself that *Traders* would be not merely the highlight of his career, but a catalyst toward stardom. If our painful discussion on opening night had left George with any false hopes, Hector's review surely snuffed them.

Where was George now? Did he need to hear from me? I should ask Manny to excuse me, then try phoning from the other room. I'd tried to call George several times Sunday after the graduation exercises, but no one answered. I would have tried the next morning before catching my train, but it was very early, and I didn't think George would appreciate being woken, regardless of the sweet things I might say.

My trip to New York was haunted by fitful thoughts. It was Monday—the morning when we wake from our deepest dreams to greet our grimmest realities—and I remembered the other Mondays that had led me to Evanstown. There was the morning last July when I first rode the train from New York and mulled my mother's death. A few weeks before that, also on Monday, a derelict jumped from the bridge in Central Park.

The thrum of the rails began to take hold, tugging me from full consciousness to a state that teeters between insight and void. My final weekend in Evanstown left me exhausted, and the train rocked beneath me like a cradle. Lulled by the monotone of steel licking steel, I closed my eyes.

And saw his smile—the derelict's oafish grin as he straddled the railing of the bridge. I heard the dull splash of his body swallowed by the lagoon, then the unnatural silence, broken only by birdsong and the horns of distant warring taxis.

Whether I awoke to the vision or simply dreamed it, I cannot say, but I saw another bridge, the long bridge that spans Evans Run. And I felt quite certainly, calmly, that George would kill himself by driving off this bridge.

I have no faith in premonitions, so the watery demise failed to alarm me. Besides—I told myself with the smug assurance of a now-acclaimed playwright—things don't happen that way. It's too neat, too pat. One Monday morning, a derelict jumps from a bridge. A year later, also on Monday, George drives off another bridge. Beginning and end, alpha and omega, conflict and resolution, tied up with ribbon. Ridiculous. Life is never so cleanly plotted.

Yet the thought persisted, and by Tuesday morning I had contrived a new worry: What car would George drive? Kiki's? He had driven it since autumn, at my own bidding. *That* would be cute. After entrusting me with her beloved red roadster, Kiki ends up dredging it from the river bottom, mud-clodded, Exhibit "A" in the juiciest suicide/sex scandal to hit drowsy little Evanstown since day one.

In my mind's eye the scene unfolded.

George leaves the house for work, jumping into the roadster, heading east toward the river. It's warm, the top is down, and George's hair is slicked back by the wind. The little car backfires apprehensively as the road narrows to cross the bridge. Without hesitation, George jerks the wheel sideways, crashing the car through the guardrail. It begins a long, graceful plummet, somersaulting in midair, ripping the water with an invasive splash. Neither car nor driver can be saved.

Stop it, I told myself, repelled more by the melodrama than by the fatality of my scenario. Time to get objective, get a grip on things. Searching my memory, I recalled concrete barricades that would prevent any such tragedy, accidental or deliberate. No car could fall from that bridge.

But a man could, couldn't he? He could drive to the middle, get out of the car, climb over the rail—as the derelict had—and step off the edge. George once called himself a living cliché; a predictable death might be perversely fulfilling.

I heard a ringing. My mind was awash with irrational frets, with a humorless recognition of the absurd. Again I heard it. My head was ringing.

"Aren't you going to answer the phone?" Manny asked. "Do you want me to get it?"

I could tell by his tone that he wondered what was wrong with me. Lost in thought, I'd drifted out of our conversation. "No, thank you, dear," I said with forced cheeriness. "I'm fine. I'll get it."

I went to the kitchen, where the phone rang on the wall, and lifted the receiver. "Yes?"

"Claire? This is Guy Anderson."

My God, I thought. "Hello, Guy. So glad you called." I felt as if an oversize chunk of apple were lodged in my throat as I asked, "How's . . . everything?"

"Not so good, I'm afraid," he said with no apparent emotion. After a long pause, he added, "George is dead."

I dropped the phone as if it had bitten me. Manny rushed from the other room. I fumbled with the cord, knocking the receiver against the wall while returning it to my ear. Manny pulled over a stool and propped me on it, then went to the sink for a glass of water. I pointed to the row of liquor bottles, feeling a strong, sudden preference for Scotch.

I said into the phone, "Guy, are you still there? Yes, I'm all right. But how . . . what happened?"

Guy began his story. "George was quiet and withdrawn all weekend. He'd been in high spirits till opening night, but when I saw him after the show, he'd changed completely. He told me Arnold Manley would be playing Jerome in New York."

Guy stopped. His mouth had gone dry. Before he could continue, I asked, "Wasn't it common knowledge about . . . New York?" I was reluctant to mention Manny by name, who at that moment handed me a much-needed cocktail.

"Sure," Guy answered, "but George was convinced he was Broadway-bound. I'd have set him straight if I'd known his whole plan, but I'm the last person he'd tell." Again he broke off, beginning to cry.

I sipped the Scotch, then told him, "Truly, Guy, I didn't know either."

"By Monday morning," he continued, "George seemed a little better and planned to go to work. He came downstairs for coffee. The *Weekly Review* had arrived, and he was anxious to read Hector Bosch's column. I suppose you've seen it."

"Yes, Guy," I said, swallowing hard.

"When he finished reading the review, he put down the paper and went back upstairs without saying a word. He was up there a long time. I couldn't hear anything and was getting nervous till I heard him turn on the shower. Finally, he dressed and came down again. He'd cut his hair."

"Christ . . ."

"Even shorter than before, a real hack-job. He grabbed his keys and headed for the door. I told him, 'You can't go to Potter's looking like that.' He wisecracked about needing to build a career—referring, I guess, to Bosch's review—then he walked out the door, got in the car, and drove away. It was the last time I saw him, Claire. He never got to Potter's."

"God, I knew it." The ice in my glass rattled as I raised it to my mouth. I slurped the whiskey, then said, "Do forgive my asking, Guy, but was he driving Kiki's car?"

"Why, no." He paused, befuddled. "He drove his own."

Awkwardly, I explained, "I thought it would make matters all the worse if Kiki's car . . . got wrecked."

"George didn't die in the car. He died in the VD clinic."

"Where?" I asked, certain I'd heard incorrectly.

"There's a gay clinic in the town where George worked. He went there because they didn't know him. He'd always used the Planned Parenthood clinic here in Evanstown for his checkups. The gay clinic didn't have his records."

"I don't understand," I mumbled. Gay clinics? Death? The specter of AIDS shifted my all-consuming dread from George's fate, already sealed, to my own.

But Guy continued, "George was allergic to penicillin. The clinic didn't know, and he didn't tell them. He told them he'd been exposed to syphilis, knowing they routinely treat it without waiting for results of a blood test. George took his shot in the ass, a massive dose of penicillin, then excused himself to the rest-room and locked himself in. His reaction must have begun at once, but they didn't know anything was wrong until ten minutes later when they heard the thrashing. They broke down the door. By the time they got to him, he was dead—strangled by the swelling in his neck."

Stunned by the story, even more bizarre than my morbid fantasies had concocted, I sat limp-shouldered and speechless.

Manny poured me a fresh drink while Guy said, "There'll be a funeral of sorts on Thursday. You're welcome to attend."

"Thank you, Guy. Of course I'll be there."

His message complete, his business done, Guy sobbed openly, rambling a bit, apologizing. I assured him through my own tears that I understood his grief because I felt it too. I offered feeble words of comfort, thanked him for delivering the painful news, and hung up.

Manny gave me the second drink and stood quietly at my side. Resting his hand on my shoulder, he suggested, "If it would help, I'll go with you."

"Thank you, baby, but no . . . ," I said with a wistful sigh. "I'll go alone." Sipping the Scotch, I brushed a tear from my chin with the back of my hand.

Then a wry, tiny smile curled my lip. George had been upstaged by Manny once too often. I repeated, "I'll go alone."

George once told me he wanted to be cremated when he died, with the ashes buried in his garden next to the remains of a weimaraner. I assumed he was joking. I was wrong.

George repeated these wishes to Guy last weekend, adding that when the time arrived, he wanted an ordained minister to emcee the rites. Guy said that no man of the cloth would bury human ashes in unhallowed ground next to a dead dog. "Then get a Unitarian," George snapped. "They'll do anything." Guy laughed. He assumed George was joking. He was wrong.

Standing by a birdbath now, I wait for the end of the prayers. An unlikely clump of mourners is gathered around a little walnut chest that sits in the grass by the dog's grave. Once displayed atop George's writing desk, the chest now contains his ashes. A Unitarian reads from a black leather book; a limp lavender ribbon hangs from its tissue-thin pages. A cocktail cart, fully stocked, is parked near the house, ready to be wheeled among the bereaved when the praying stops. George's passing will be toasted as well as mourned.

I openly stare at the others in the garden, amused by their chagrin when, one by one, they raise their bowed heads to peek at me, only to find my eyes already aimed at theirs. Most are wearing black, as I am. Our grim attire clashes with the profusion of flowers, the prettiness of life.

Among the mourners, Kiki is conspicuous for the dazzle of her costume. With its sequined veil and yards of black gossamer, it could have been pilfered from the Queen of the Night. President Henry is least conspicuous, dressed, as always, like a pallbearer. The Garamonds are here, Paul and Connie—he, out of season, in his usual tweeds—she, in a sensible black dress. Guy is standing near the minister, holding up well. George's psychiatrist is also present, emotionless to the point of looking smug. One would assume his professional self-confidence would be shaken on such an occasion, but he has learned to live with failure in a way that his patient did not. The psychiatrist is accompanied by his vapid lover, Nigel Slough, who shifts his weight from foot to foot, poking the earth, bored by the whole business. There is an older man, dignified though effeminate, who must be Neil Potter, George's boss. There are others I don't recognize, including two women—one middle-aged, the other a teen—who appear to be mother and daughter. Both are pretty; both look uncomfortable. Could this be George's ex-wife and child? I decide they are, discerning George's features in the girl.

I study the ex-wife and look within her eyes, knowing we have shared George's pleasures. I wonder if her years without him have been happy or bitter. How has she dealt with frustration, deprived of his animal talents? And Guy. He has known, better than anyone, the power of George's passion. Guy will surely "cope," but I doubt if he will ever quell the longing. And what of the others, the nameless bereaved? Who among them shared George with me? Who among them gasped as I did when he first revealed his endowment?

Do not be shocked by these carnal dotings. They spring from sudden loss, an unpleasant train trip, and the heat of the day. Both the setting and the circumstances seem unreal. The first time I left Evanstown, it took thirty years to return. The next time I left, I came back in three days—to bury a friend who chose to die because his dreams were broken.

George once told me that he talked to himself in the shower, indulging in fantasies or rehearsing his day. I do the same—not in the shower, but during any robbed moments of introspection—as I am doing now. But why? What are we rehearsing?

In the theater, we try to create an image of life that's meaningful, beautiful, or even profound. But I wonder if our rehearsing doesn't void our vision. We can rehearse a play, but we can't rehearse life. We can never go back and tamper with a scene, tinker with a line. We only improvise.

George was an actor. He dreamed up a role for himself and honed it to perfection. But he didn't have a script—only a plan, a scheme he shared with no one. When his big scene arrived, he stood alone on a bare stage while his dreams dissolved like distant applause.

I came to Evanstown to write a play. I wrote about George because his confusion helped identify my own. I packaged that confusion in a character called Jerome. I gave George the role, taught him Jerome's speeches, even dressed him in Jerome's clothes, but George never saw himself beneath the costume. He proved his lack of understanding when he took his own life. Remarkably, clarity sprang from the grayness of his delusions, igniting for me the truth of the words I had written.

Whether in affairs of the heart or of finance, we act as traders. Expecting to take as well as to give, we are traders. George, like so many, could never face this elusive truth.

How did he delude himself? Not by believing that he could be a star—perhaps he could have been. No, his deadly dream was that *I owed him* stardom.

Had I known, as I feared, that the events of last weekend left George on the brink of suicide, I would have tried to reason with him, dissuade him, save him—but I would not have cast him on Broadway. Manny will star in New York because he is the far better actor. Reality can't be simply denied and wished away. George tried. He was destined to fail.

Does his death lend any meaning to the lives of those gathered for these rites? I think not. They sniffle and sob, lost in the luxury of grief.

It would be fitting if I could summon a tear and participate more fully in this drama, but I cannot. I did my crying two days ago when I received the news. The others surely marvel at how well I'm holding up. What they fail to realize is that I'm not grieving at all. My mourning was brief and sincere—George was a friend, and it was painful to imagine his suffering. But my grief has given way to the quiet, palpable joy of insight.

The Unitarian has stopped praying, and the silence breaks my thoughts. All eyes follow Guy as he steps forward to kneel at the tiny grave. He places the burled box in the ground, then covers it with handfuls of earth. A neat square of sod is pulled over it like a blanket. With a few loving tucks, George's burial is complete.

I once thought my ultimate act of maturity would be to bury my mother. George, it seems, has taken her place. I should give her a call next week. She'll wonder where I've been. Besides, we need to talk.

Bowed heads turn, stealing sidelong glimpses of the cocktail cart as it rattles toward the center of the garden.

❑